THE WAGON WARS

Also by James A. Ritchie

The Last Free Range
Kerrigan
The Payback
Over on the Lonesome Side

THE WAGON WARS

James A. Ritchie

Walker and Company
New York

First published in the United States of America in 1997 by Walker Publishing
Company, Inc.

Published simultaneously in Canada by Thomas Allen & Son Canada,
Limited, Markham, Ontario

Library of Congress Cataloging-in-Publication Data
Ritchie, James A.
The wagon wars / James A. Ritchie.
p.   cm.
ISBN 0-8027-4157-6
I. Title.
PS3568.I814W34   1997
813'.54—dc20   96-43383
CIP

Printed in the United States of America

2   4   6   8   10   9   7   5   3   1

CHAPTER 1

WHEN BILLY MARTIN, Johnny Stevens, and I rode into Arizona looking for a place to settle, we had more money between us than we'd ever seen, a bit over three thousand dollars all told. But finding a likely spot wasn't as easy as a body would think. For one thing, three thousand was scant for the kind of place we wanted, and each time we stopped in town to look around, a bit more went for food, whiskey, and the occasional saloon woman. And when you're lookin' for something without knowing exactly what it is, it can be a mite hard to find.

And the truth of it is, each of us might have been looking for different things. Me, I was on the downhill side of forty-five and was looking more than anything for a place where I could spend the rest of my life in peace. For my part, what I wanted was a little blacksmith shop where I could earn a living and still have a bit of time to sit around and drink with the boys, and the money to buy some fancies for any upstairs gal that caught my eye.

Johnny Stevens was in his late twenties, still young enough to be full of piss and vinegar and to look on trouble as some kind of adventure. But he was old enough and wise enough to know it was an adventure that could kill you.

Billy Martin, now, well, he was the youngest of us, and the hardest to figure. Billy had a wooden leg that he'd carved himself after he lost his leg back in Texas. He got shot when the three of us stumbled into a range war.

Thing is, that wooden leg had its effect on Billy. He took losing his leg as well as anybody I'd known, and back dur-

1

ing the war I'd seen legs and arms stacked up six feet high outside the surgeons' tents.

But Billy was simply dead set on proving a wooden leg didn't make him any less a man. If there was a difficult thing to be done, Billy was the first to try it, and more often than not he did it well. Thing is, trying to prove he was still a whole man made him try things another man would back away from, and with good cause.

The point of all this being, we each had our reasons for looking toward fresher pastures, and we each had our own ideas as to what we wanted. About all we knew for certain was we all wanted a place where the barbed wire might be a while catching up to us, somewhere a man could live as he wanted so long as he didn't step on nobody else's toes.

Arizona wasn't the safest place for three men to go riding the wild country. For a time, it seemed the Apache trouble was mostly over, but now Geronimo and some of his band were running loose. The army said he didn't have more than twenty-five or thirty warriors with him, and promised a capture any day.

Not many believed the army. Even if Geronimo didn't have more than thirty warriors, it was by damn certain his wasn't the only group of Apaches out there in the mountains. Raids were coming way the hell too close together in time and too far apart in distance for one small band to be doing all the army claimed it was.

Not that Apaches were responsible for all the hell-raising going on. Leaving them out of it altogether, a man could still run into more trouble than he could rightly handle. As Texas and New Mexico became more settled, the outlaws and gunhands there began drifting into Arizona. Tack on Mexican banditos who came across the border to rustle cattle, rob stages, and generally play hob, and you can see why there were safer places to be.

We didn't let that stop us none, though we did try to avoid the real trouble spots. Most were down there in the southeastern corner of Arizona. Not that a body could feel safe anywhere in the territory, but those mountains down around the San Carlos Indian Reservation were about the worst, though the border country was as bad.

Still, after a good bit of drifting, that's the direction we headed. Then we came down the Verde River, and right away we all knew we wanted to stop somewhere within riding distance of that country.

I swear, you never saw such country. The Verde itself wasn't much of a river, I reckon . . . just a not-too-wide, not-too-deep ribbon of water taking its own time getting where it was going. But, by God, the country around it made a man sit up and take notice. Mostly it was green and growing, though given to change all of a sudden. A man could go from wet and green to dry and burning-hot in only a few hours, and not work his horse into a sweat in the riding.

The Mazatzal Mountains squatted around the Verde, and the Mogollon Plateau wasn't too many miles due east of where we stopped to look around. Prescott was thirty or thirty-five miles west and maybe twenty or so north. Phoenix was no more than eighty miles south and a handful of miles west.

Time we came down to the Salt River, we were looking for a place to stay. Thing was, if we wanted to start up a blacksmith shop, we needed a town. Phoenix wasn't much, but even that was a bit bigger and a bit too settled for our liking. But it was a town, so we decided to stay over a few days while we thought things over.

Come nightfall, me and Johnny got ourselves into a low-stakes poker game, and Billy cut a pretty filly from the small herd of saloon girls. When he came back downstairs two hours later, the poker game had broken up, and me an' Johnny were sipping beer at a corner table.

Billy stopped by the bar, brought a beer over, and joined us. "Might have tied onto something," he said.

"Looked like something fine to me," Johnny said. "Might be I'll see how hard she bucks, myself."

Billy grinned, shook his head. "You want her to buck, you best wear your spurs. She talks pretty good, though."

"I don't aim to pay for talk," Johnny said. "I get more'n enough talk from you two."

"Ain't neither of us got a voice that sweet. Besides, it's what she had to say that interested me. Seems Jenny, that's her name, just came over from a town name of Globe a couple of weeks back.

"She said the only blacksmith in town was looking to sell out—lock, stock, and anvil. As of two weeks back, he didn't have any takers."

"How'd she know about it?" I asked.

"He was one of her best customers. Fellow's name is Dick Mathers. His wife caught him sneaking up to see Jenny and lit out for back east somewhere. He wants to follow, but needs cash."

"Sounds good on the surface," Johnny said. "I've heard of Globe, but I can't say I know exactly where it is."

"It's just this side of the San Carlos Reservation," Billy said. " 'Bout a hundred miles straight east, Jenny said. She said it's a big enough town to be safe, and small enough so as not to make a man feel crowded."

Me an' Johnny looked at each other. Johnny shrugged. "Why not?" he said.

We stayed the night in Phoenix, then set out for Globe at first light, following along the Butterfield stage route. We hadn't been on the trail more than three days when we saw smoke up ahead a good piece. Shucking our rifles and spreading out a little, we rode ahead.

It was early on to spring, and the sun was warm shining down on us, but a chill went through me as we rode. Once a man's seen trouble a few times, he learns to smell it in the air. The way Billy and Johnny's faces looked, they had the same feeling.

That column of smoke up ahead meant trouble. It was too big to be any kind of campfire, and too small and thick to be a brushfire. No, sir. Something was burning that ought not to have been, and that likely meant somebody had run into hard luck.

The brush was thick along the road, and even after we rode to within forty or fifty yards of the smoke, we still couldn't see the cause. We sat there a time, rifles in hand, looking over the country. "You boys stay here and keep an eye out," I said.

Gently touching my spurs to my big dun-colored gelding, I went on ahead. Truth is, I didn't much trust that horse. His name was Shanghai . . . that was his name when I bought him, and he was a used-to-be stallion that didn't seem to know he'd been cut. The one time I'd fired a weapon from off his back—to kill a rattlesnake—he went to bucking.

The last thing in the world I wanted was to be on the back of a bucking horse should somebody start shooting at me, so midway to that smoke, I climbed down and went ahead on foot, leading Shanghai behind me. I was near on the smoke before I could make out what was burning.

Twenty yards off the road, the remains of a still burning wagon sent smoke high into the air. A bit of the brush near the wagon was trying to catch fire, but we'd already had a couple of spring rains, and the brush held enough water to fight off the fire.

I looped Shanghai's reins around some brush close to the road, then stepped over into the brush. It was then I saw the first body. It was that of a man, lying facedown in the dirt. He wore a black broadcloth suit, made darker by the blood soaking it. Easing over to him, I felt for a pulse and found none. He hadn't been dead long.

The second body was lying twenty feet from the first. This one was a woman. Her bodice was torn open, her skirt hiked up about her waist, and the remains of her unmentionables scattered about. Her wrists and ankles were bruised nearly black by the strong hands that had held her.

She, too, was dead. The two bullet holes in her chest were made by a pistol held right against the skin, by the looks of the powder burns. Swallowing hard, I turned away from the sight.

Whoever had murdered those folks couldn't be far away. The fire on the wagon was just beginning to die down, and a wagon that size wouldn't burn long . . . at least not enough to put up such a column of smoke. Half an hour, I'd say. Maybe less.

A bee buzzed past my head and lost itself in the brush, meaning we couldn't be far from water. Somewhere in the distance a quail gave out its gathering call. Johnny and Billy would be wondering about me, but there was nothing for it. There was a good chance that whoever had done all this had left a man or two behind just to see who might be drawn to the smoke, and moving would be a sure way to let them know my position.

So I waited, trying not to move at all. I didn't even move my head, but let my eyes scan the brush. Five minutes passed and my back began to hurt. Still I didn't move.

It was then something moved yonder in the brush. The sound of cloth rubbing against brush came first to my ears, followed by the sound of a small stick breaking. Moving quickly back into some thicker cover, I knelt down on one knee and waited.

Then I saw a flash of color—just the quickest flicker of something bright. Still I didn't move. And then, so quick it took me by surprise, a figure stepped into the open not forty feet in front of me. Pure reflex snapped the rifle to my shoulder and thumbed back the hammer.

I don't know how I kept from firing, but thank goodness in the last hundredth of a second I took my finger off the trigger and swung the rifle out of line. The figure was that of a little boy, no more'n five or six. The whole front of his once white shirt was now red with blood, and the side of his face was a solid, swollen bruise, but he was alive.

Without warning, he crumpled and fell. I ran to him, swept the small body into my arms, and carried him back to the road. In seconds, Johnny and Billy were there, swinging off their horses before they'd come to a stop.

Easing the boy down in the road, I dropped back a second to catch my breath before kneeling down to examine the boy. Johnny beat me to it. He opened the boy's shirt, wiped blood away with his bandanna.

"Looks like somebody clubbed him with something, then shot him," Johnny said. "It don't look too bad, but he's lost a lot of blood."

I looked at the wound. The bullet had cut right between the muscle at the top of his shoulder and the bone beneath. It was a nasty wound, but if we could get the bleeding stopped, and if it didn't fester up, he'd likely live.

Johnny folded his bandanna and tied it across the wound, then we went looking for a place to camp. We found a water hole not far off the trail, and there we built a small fire. Johnny bathed and cleaned the boy's shoulder and a cut in his scalp that I'd not noticed.

"Somebody clubbed him a good one," Johnny said. "And not with his fist. The whole side of his face is swollen and there's a knot over his ear the size of a goose egg."

"Who'd do a thing like that, Ben? You reckon it was Apaches?"

I shrugged. "Wasn't no time to look around, nor to read sign. If you can do without me, I guess I'll go back over and do just that. Might as well dig a couple of graves whilst I'm at it, if I can find a shovel."

"You go on ahead," Johnny said. "There's nothing you can do here, and I'd as soon not move him till morning. No, you go on ahead. It's early yet, but I may as well make coffee and get out the frying pan."

Standing up, I started away. Billy hopped up and said,

"I'll go along, Ben. Looking at that boy is more than I can take."

"It's no better back at the wagon," I said, "but come along if you can stomach it."

Leaving our horses where they were, I took my blanket under my arm, and me and Billy walked back down and across the road. We were still on edge, and we both carried rifles. Men who'd done the kind of thing these had wouldn't hesitate a minute to try to kill us.

But right then, walking down toward that wagon, knowing the sight that awaited us, I was more'n half hoping they would come riding back. Men like that didn't deserve to live no more than a rattlesnake.

We walked through the brush, and Billy had his first look at the woman. She was lying just as I'd found her. Billy's face flushed red, then went pale. Turning away from the body and dropping to his knees, he heaved up everything he'd eaten all day long.

CHAPTER 2

WHILE BILLY WAS unloading his stomach, I straightened out the woman's body, drug the man over beside her, then covered both bodies with my blanket. Then I started looking around. There were papers, gear, and other things from the wagon strewn about, but not wanting to track up the area before I read the sign, I spent a few minutes looking around.

I hadn't been at it more than a few minutes when Billy came over beside me. His face was still pale, and when he ran the back of his hand over his mouth, I could see he was shaking.

"I'm sorry, Ben," he said. "It was the woman. I never saw anything like that."

"No need to be sorry. First dead man I ever saw was a friend of mine named Arnold Denny. We joined up and went off to war together, and not long after we were marching side by side toward a union line.

"Arnold turned to me like he was going to say something, and right then a big piece of shrapnel hit him in the side of the head. It sliced his face off, but for what seemed like a long time he stood there.

"Then he made this gurgling sound in his throat and fell forward. I caught him, eased him down. He was already dead. Not ten seconds later I did just like you."

"Honest?"

"Yes, sir. Hadn't been for a sergeant who was following along, I might have tried running all the way back home, too. I was sure thinking about it.

"Only that sergeant must have known what was going

9

through my mind. He jerked me up by the scruff of my neck and shoved my musket back into my hands and pushed me toward the front of the line. That big sergeant was an Irishman named Black McConnell, and just knowing he was back there somewhere was all that got me through the day. He was killed at the Third Battle of Winchester."

"I never heard you talk much about the war," Billy said. "I always wondered why."

"There ain't many pleasant memories associated with it, I guess. Most of the men I hear gabbering about the war never saw action themselves. There was forty thousand men killed or wounded at Gettysburg alone.

"There just ain't nothing about the war that I recall fondly, 'cept some of the men I knew."

Billy nodded, looked at the ground. "You figured out who did this yet?"

"Wasn't Indians. That's about all I can say."

"How do you know?"

"Look for yourself. Every manjack here was wearing boots, and most had spurs strapped on." I pointed to one track in particular. "This one was wearing spurs with a drop shank and big rowels.

"See how clear-cut his heel track is? New boots, likely. Else he don't walk no more'n he has to. His spurs still drag the ground with every step. Don't look like more than four points on them, neither."

"Man who wears spurs like that don't care nothing for a horse," Billy said.

I nodded. As a rule, the fewer the points on a rowel, the more they poked into the flesh of a horse. Most cowhands wore sunset or flower-petal spurs with small points all the way around. And even then, if a man cared for his horse, he'd take a file and dull the points even more.

Spurs were meant to get a horse's attention, and that's all. Spurs like this fellow was wearing could draw blood and scar a horse permanent. There simply wasn't ever a need for it. But then there's no reason to think any man who was brutal enough to kill and maim a young family would think twice about misusing a horse.

We followed the tracks to a dry camp a couple of hundred yards back in the brush. The camp itself was in a small draw where it couldn't be seen from the road, but there was a spot not far away where a body could climb up on some rock and see the road for a good piece in either direction. From the tracks, it looked like several of the men had taken turns doing just that.

We found where they'd tied their horses, and counted an even dozen sets of tracks. From the clear, sharp track they left, it was my guess all the horses but two had been shod recently. There were a couple of nicks and marks in the shoes that I'd likely recognize should I see them again, though likely I wouldn't.

Most horses were shod every month or thereabouts, and once they were wearing new horseshoes, there'd be a whole new set of nicks and marks.

Walking back to where they'd built their fire, I poked around in the ashes with a stick. Red coals glowed beneath.

From the depth of the ashes, it appeared the men had camped there for at least two days. And then had left in a hurry once they were done with the murder and rape.

Once we'd seen all there was to see, me and Billy walked back to the wagon. Only then did we go through the scattered belongings. The wagon hadn't been heavily loaded, but there was enough clothing about to make it look like those folks were taking a fair-sized trip.

I couldn't find a wallet anywhere, even after going through the man's clothing, but I did find enough papers to give me an idea as to who the man was. I found three letters addressed to a Trent Smalley, and then a letter from the president of a bank in Globe.

The letter was addressed "To Whom It May Concern,"

and was actually a letter of introduction that the man I took to be Smalley was carrying. Nothing I could find gave me the name of the woman or the boy.

Billy did find a locket with a silver chain. It was lying back under the wagon, but though the clasp was broken, the fire hadn't hurt it none. Opening the locket, we found a tiny photograph of the family, though the boy had obviously been a couple of years younger when the photograph was taken.

There was no shovel anywhere about the wagon, and we had nothing at all to dig with. For lack of anything better, we covered the bodies with rocks until someone could ride back out and bury them proper.

By the time we returned to Johnny and the boy, supper was ready and the boy was as patched up as Johnny could make him. "He hasn't stirred, nor even made a sound," Johnny said. "I got a good bit of water down him, though. I was afraid to try food, for fear he'd choke."

"We got anything to make soup of?"

"Beans, I reckon. Take 'em a good while to simmer down. I'd have to simmer them in a skillet, at that."

"Nothing else?"

"No, I—wait a minute." Johnny walked over to where he'd laid his saddlebags. Reaching inside, he came out with a tin of peaches.

"Where'd you get those?" Billy asked.

"Back in Phoenix. Got a couple more cans in there. Figured we'd have them for a treat this side of Globe somewhere. Don't know if the boy'll be able to swallow any of the peaches, but the juice might do him some good."

Johnny opened the can with his knife, poured some of the juice in a tin cup. Gently lifting the boy's head, he poured a little juice into the small mouth. Some came back out and dribbled down his chin, but most got swallowed.

There wasn't anything else we could do. Globe was the closest town we knew of, but even that was almost as far away as Phoenix, by our reckoning. With the shape the boy was in, we'd need a travois to get him there, and hauling him behind a horse like that would be a slow thing.

We slept right there. Next morning I was up with the sun, putting on a fresh pot of coffee, when the boy woke up. Hearing a kind of grunt, I looked over. The boy was sitting up, his eyes wide and staring. His eyes settled on me, and he started screaming.

Billy and Johnny both sat bolt upright. Running over to the boy, I knelt down. Weak as he had to be, the boy tried to scurry away. Not knowing what else to do, I took hold of him and held him to me.

"It's all right, boy," I said. "Ain't nobody going to hurt you. It's all right."

The boy continued to struggle for a minute, then went limp. He started crying, and for a time I sat there with him. Children were as strange to me as anything on earth. I didn't have no idea of what to do or say.

Just holding him and talking soft seemed to help though. I'd done the same thing with hurt dogs a time or two, and it seemed to work out. Though one time a dog I was trying to comfort bit me good. He didn't mean it, I figured, and kept on holding him.

Finally the boy stopped crying. Making eye contact with him, I found my voice catching in my throat. "Are you all right, son?"

His eyes were still wet and his voice was weak. "My head hurts," he said. "My head hurts real bad."

He closed his eyes and dropped back off just like that. From his breathing, it seemed he was asleep rather than unconscious. Easing him back down on the blanket, I stood up.

An hour later, we got lucky. Me and Johnny were down by the road, looking for proper poles to make a travois, when we saw dust way down the road a piece. An object grew in the dust, turned into a stagecoach. Stepping out into the middle of the road, I held up both hands to flag it down.

The driver pulled the horses up short, but the guard thumbed back the hammers of the shotgun he held. "Who are you," he asked, "and what do you want?"

"My name is Ben Hawkins," I said. "That's Johnny Stevens over there. Look, we have a wounded boy back in the brush apiece. He needs a doctor."

"A boy?"

"Yes, sir. No more'n seven or eight, I'd say."

I could see him thinking. "Mister," he said, "I don't mean to slight your word, but I don't know you from Adam. Might be one of you ought to go get the boy while the other stays here in sight."

"That's fair enough. Johnny, go on back."

Johnny walked off into the brush, and while he was gone I explained what had happened. A man with fat jowls stuck his head out the coach window and asked what the holdup was. "Ain't no holdup," the driver yelled down. "Just you hold your water."

Johnny and Billy came back out of the brush, the boy in Johnny's arms. He was awake, but still looked limp as a rag doll. As soon as the boy saw me, he stretched out his arms and started struggling. Johnny handed him to me.

"That boy looks almighty bad," the driver said. "Put him in the coach and we'll get him to Globe as quick as we can."

Opening the door to the stage, I tried to put the boy inside. He wouldn't turn loose of my neck. "Might be you'd better ride along with him," the driver said. "Seems he's taken a shine to you.

"You two best follow along. Folks in Globe will want to hear the story from you, I expect."

"That's where we were heading anyway," Billy said. "You go on ahead. We'll break camp and follow as soon as we can. Ben, you want us to tie your horse behind the stage, or bring him along when we come?"

"Bring him along," I said. "Likely we won't beat you there by much."

The only passengers in the stage were the man with the fat face and a prim-looking, well-dressed woman of about fifty. Settling in next to the woman, I tried to make myself comfortable.

"Rest his feet on my lap," the woman said. "I'm afraid this stage is pretty rough."

She was right. Even on the smoothest sections, it wasn't the easiest ride I'd ever had, and now and again we hit bumps that near shook my teeth loose. The boy kept his face against my chest. He moaned a little from time to time, and almost yelled when we hit real bumps. About the third or fourth time it happened, the fat man snorted.

"Can't you keep that boy quiet?"

"No, sir," I said. "But I got a ten-dollar gold piece that says I can throw you out the door if you open *your* mouth again."

He looked into my eyes, and whatever he saw there told him I meant it. He didn't look none too happy, but he never said another word the rest of the trip.

Globe was a bit bigger than I'd figured it would be. The main drag was lined with businesses, and I figured there must have been several hundred folks lived there. Maybe up to eight hundred or a thousand, all told. And it seemed half of them came running when the stage tore into town.

The stage driver jerked the horses to a stop, jumped down, and opened the door of the coach. Once I eased out, he pointed to a flight of stairs leading up the side of a building to a door. "Don't know if he's in," the driver said, "but that's the only doctor's office for a hundred miles."

Carrying the boy up the steps, I tried the door. It opened and I stepped inside. A man I took to be the doctor was sitting at a desk, reading a thick book. Soon as he saw me, he put down the book, came around, and took the boy from me. Leading the way into a back room, he put the boy on a bed and went to examining him.

He asked me questions as he worked, and I told him

what had happened as best I knew. His name was Doctor Jefferies, and while he didn't look old enough to be much of anything, he seemed to know his business.

Once I'd told Dr. Jefferies all I knew, he asked me to wait out in the office. I went on out, just in time to meet the town marshal coming in. He shook my hand, said his name was Sam Reynolds, and I had to tell my story all over again.

Once he had my story, Marshal Reynolds went in to see the boy, then came back out. "That's Trent's boy, all right," he said. "His name is Todd. He ain't but seven. His mother's name was Melissa.

"They hadn't been in Globe but a few months, but I guess everybody in town knew them. Good folks.

"The truth is, there's not much I can do about what happened out there, but I'll get in touch with the army. Likely they'll want to talk to you. Were you planning on staying in Globe long?"

"That all depends," I said. "Someone told us there might be a smithy for sale. Me an' my friends were riding over to take a look."

Marshal Reynolds grinned. "That's true enough. Jess Mathers has been trying to sell his place ever since his wife took off.

"Trouble is, a smithy isn't worth a thing unless a man knows the business. And that place of Mathers's isn't much for looks. He's let it run down considerably. I'd say you could get it for a song. His smithy is right down at the east end of town, but like as not you'll find Jess at one saloon or another."

I nodded. "I'll look him up soon as the doc lets me know how the boy is."

Marshal Reynolds left, and twenty minutes later I was still waiting. Then the outside door opened again and a pretty young woman came in carrying a big tray of food.

"Is your name Ben Hawkins?" she asked.

"Yes, ma'am."

She set the tray down on a small table. "Then this is yours," she said. "Sam . . . Marshal Reynolds said you had to be hungry after riding that stage all afternoon."

"He was right about that. How much do I owe you?"

"It's already taken care of. He said it was the least he could do after the way you helped the boy. How is he?"

"I don't know yet, ma'am."

"My name is Charlotte Reynolds," she said. "The marshal is my husband. Would you let us know as soon as you learn anything?"

"Yes, ma'am. First thing. And thank your husband for the food. My stomach was starting to think my throat had been cut."

She smiled, and a pretty sight it was. Marshal Reynolds was a lucky man. "I'll tell him."

She left and I lifted the lid off the tray. You never saw such a pile of fried chicken, mashed potatoes, green beans, and bread. A big cup of coffee was also under there, and I sipped at it. Still boiling hot, and strong enough to peel paint. Just right.

I had nearly all the food inside my belly when Doc Jefferies came out. "Well, he's going to live," he said. "But I'm still worried about him. Do you know if he saw what happened to his parents?"

"I can't say, doc. But he saw the results, I think."

"Well, his body will heal quickly . . . Somebody did a fine job dressing his wound. It's his mind I'm worried about.

"Still, some children are resilient. We'll just have to wait and see."

"Is he awake?"

"No. I gave him a little laudanum for the pain. It'll make him sleep, and I want to keep him that way until morning. When he does wake up, I want his first thoughts to be about food.

"He may want to see you, as well. Since you were the first

to comfort him, you may be the only one he really trusts
for some time to come."

"Me? I don't know anything about children."

"You know enough, Mr. Hawkins. You did exactly the
right thing in holding him as you did. It may have made
all the difference. I don't know who the boy will end up
staying with, but whoever it is, you should visit him as often
as possible, at least for a time."

"I reckon I can, but are you sure it'll help? That boy
don't know me from nothing."

"He knows you were there when it mattered, Mr. Hawkins. That's all that counts."

Not knowing what else to say, I nodded, then stuck a
thumb toward the tray the food came on. "Marshal Reynolds' wife brought that up," I said. "If you know whereabouts it came from, I can get it out of your office."

Doc Jefferies smiled. "It's from Molly's. If you're going
that way, would you ask Molly to bring me a tray? She'll
know what to put on it, and I hate to leave the boy alone
just yet."

"Yes, sir. I sure will. And you let me know what it costs
to care for the boy. I can afford to pay."

"Thank you. On both counts. Molly's is right across the
street and west about a block."

Taking the tray out, I walked down and found Molly's. It
was a pretty little restaurant with red-and-white-checkered
tablecloths and curtains to match. Molly herself was a bru-
nette whose hair was now streaked with gray, and the wrin-
kles of her face showed a lifetime spent smiling.

She took the tray and promised to take some food to
Doc Jefferies. I went out, stood on the boardwalk for a
minute, then decided to walk about town to see how it
stacked up against what I'd been looking for.

Stopping in at a store, I picked up a handful of cigars,
stuck all but one in my pocket, and lit that one. Taking a
good puff to get it going, I started walking.

CHAPTER 3

MARSHAL REYNOLDS SAW me walking along and crossed the street to ask me about the boy. I told him what Doc Jefferies said and thanked him for the food. He waved it off. "If you're wanting to see Jess Mathers," he said, "now would be the time. He's down there at his shop and seems sober. You won't find him that way often."

I was about to answer when Marshal Reynolds turned his eyes away. "Couple of riders coming in," he said.

Looking that way, I saw them. "Those are my partners. The one on the left is Billy Martin. The other is Johnny Stevens."

They saw me and came riding over. Billy had an easier job getting down than Johnny. I introduced both to Marshal Reynolds, who shook their hands. We all talked a spell, then Marshal Reynolds went about his business.

I told them about the blacksmith shop, and we decided to go down that way after putting up the horses. The livery was at the opposite end of town, but that still wasn't much of a walk, and in no more than fifteen minutes we had the horses boarded and were on our way to see Jess Mathers.

We met him coming out as we were going in. Mathers wasn't a tall man, but he had a barrel chest and arms like a bear. He also had bloodshot eyes, a red, veined nose of the kind a man gets from drinking too much whiskey, and a belly that was pushing its way toward bursting.

Mathers didn't seem any too happy to see us at first. "I'm closing for the day," he said. "If you have work that needs doing, try me tomorrow."

"Didn't come for work," I said. "We heard you might want to sell the place."

That caught his attention. He hauled up so sudden his feet skidded in the soft dirt. "Well, now," he said. "That's a different story. Yes, sir. I am looking to sell . . . if the price is right."

"Haven't got much to spend," I said, "and it's not really my line anyway. But we're looking for something to keep us busy. Mind if we have a look around?"

"Mind? Not a bit. Let me show you the place. It needs a little work, but it's a money-maker for the right man."

We looked around. There wasn't all that much to see. Mathers had tools and iron stock in plenty, but the tools were scattered around, and many showed rust. The building itself had three rooms: the big front work area, a good-sized storage room, and a smaller room with two cots, a little table, and two chairs.

There was also a stable built onto the back of the smithy, though it had only four stalls. At one time it must have been a fine smithy. It no longer had much going for it.

From the looks of it, the building had never been painted, and many of the wall boards were warped enough to let light in from the outside. The roof, too, showed light here and there, and the whole place was filthy. The stalls hadn't been cleaned in a month of Sundays.

"What are you asking?" I said.

Mathers started to say something, closed his mouth, tried again. "Twenty-five hundred and I just walk away."

I shook my head. "At that price, we'll be walking. I don't mean to badmouth you, Mr. Mathers, but you've let this place run to seed. For that kind of money I could buy new tools, and put up a building around them. No, sir. A man would be a fool to pay a quarter what you're askin', and you know it."

"It ain't just for what you see. There's half a dozen head of fine horses out back. They ought to be worth seven, eight hundred, anyway."

"Let's have a look."

We went out back. The horses were good stock. They might even have been worth what he claimed. "I won't argue with you about them," I said. "But that's a long way from making up the difference. I'll give you a thousand dollars. Horses, tools, everything. That's the best I can do."

His face fell. "I'll tell you the truth," he said. "I know what this place is worth, and your price ain't far off. But I got to have fifteen hundred, or it'll do me no good to sell. I owe money here, and I'll need cash to start over somewhere else.

"Look, I have a house about three miles south of town. I don't use it much on account of the trouble we've had hereabouts, but it's in better shape than the smithy.

"There's a barn, a big corral, and I hold title to about twenty acres of land. It won't do me no good back east, and that's sure where I'm heading. Give me the fifteen hundred I need, and it's all yours. I'd say that's more than fair."

"Let us talk it over a minute."

"Sure. Take your time."

Me, Billy, and Johnny walked off a piece. Billy took off his hat and scratched his head. "You're the one that knows about such things," he said, "but it seems to me the main thing this place needs is about a month of hard labor. If that other place he's throwing in is any good, I'm all for it."

Johnny took out the makings and started to build a cigarette. He licked the paper, curled the end, stuck it in his mouth, and lit it. "You two are the smithies," he said. "I figured to do more horse hunting than anything. Thought maybe to sell a few through whatever place we set up, if you all agree. This would give me the chance to do just that. I say we ride out and look at his land. If it's all he says, then I'm for it."

We walked back over and told Mathers. "There's still time to ride out tonight," he said.

Billy frowned. "Our horses are wore to a frazzle."

"We can use mine," Mathers said. "There's saddles for each in the storage room there. You'd be surprised how many people ride the stage into town, then want to rent a horse. If a man could afford a nice buggy or two, he might make a tidy profit."

"Doesn't the livery rent?"

"Yes, sir. But not cheap, and not in plenty. They have one buggy and two horses to let."

We saddled up some horses, and the three of us followed him outside of town. It didn't take long to reach his land, but even before we were there, we knew the horses were fine stock. Might be they needed a week or two of grain feeding, and they needed to be run a bit, but they were fine.

The house and land Mathers showed us was up to snuff as well. The house had six rooms, was built of mortared rock and adobe, and had glass windows and a wood floor. "I built it for my wife," he said. "Guess she didn't like it."

From what Billy had been told, the house hadn't been the reason his wife took off, but that was none of my business.

The barn needed some work, and one end of the corral would have to be rebuilt, but all in all, it wasn't a bad place. And while twenty acres of land wasn't much, there was quite a bit of free range beyond. "Mr. Mathers," I said, "if you can be at the bank when it opens tomorrow, you got yourself a deal."

"I'll be there," he said.

We rode back into Globe, and I hunted around for rooms while Billy and Johnny ate their fill down at Molly's. I found a boardinghouse and took the only two rooms they had open, paying two days in advance. I figured we'd be living in that house out yonder soon as possible.

Next morning we signed the papers, paid the cash, and then the hard work began. The blacksmith shop was the money-maker, but we had to close it up in order to get everything in order before starting business. It took longer than we figured.

First thing we did was sweep the place out. Then we shoveled out the horse stalls, cleaned the tools, and ripped off every board that needed replacing. That done, we patched the roof, nailed up new wall boards, and painted the whole building a dark brown.

By the time we were finished, Mathers himself wouldn't have recognized the place. Then the subject of a sign came up. After some discussion, we came up with one that read simply: GLOBE SMITHY. Below this, in smaller letters, were the words HAWKINS, MARTIN, & STEVENS, PROPRIETORS.

Almost as an afterthought, we made up a smaller sign and hung it by the door. It read: WE RENT SADDLE HORSES.

The livery down at the other end of town wasn't much on size, and they didn't do any smithy work at all, so we planned to build on, adding eight or ten stalls when time permitted, figuring to take as much business from them as possible. But for the present, we'd done plenty, and near the moment we opened our doors for business, folks came flocking.

The next month seemed to fly past, and we soon settled in and came to know Globe.

Globe wasn't growing much, but it sure had a lot of folks coming through. Most were headed for Phoenix, or were planning to go on through to California. Now and again a family settled in, or a few copper miners drifted in, hoping to strike it rich, but like I said, most were going on through.

Traveling was mostly safe if you were with a large enough group, and most were smart enough to wait until they had twenty or more wagons before starting down the trail. Even then, there were sporadic attacks . . . usually just potshots taken from the cover of rocks.

A fellow name of P. G. Murphy had himself a good-sized freighting outfit. His main office was there in Globe, back down beside the stockyard, and now and again I ran into him somewhere around town.

Folks all called him "P. G." and he was a well-known fellow. P. G. stood six-four or thereabouts, and must have weighed a solid two-forty. He had a big mustache, a loud way of talking, and a reputation for being able to handle any of his muleskinners with his fists.

I was no freighter, but I knew enough about men to know that was saying something. Muleskinners tend to be big men who love to drink and fight. Being able to handle such men with your fists meant you were a tough man, no two ways about it. About all else I knew about P.G. Murphy was that he was from New York. He seemed to be happy as a possum in a persimmon tree over how dangerous the trails were. What with the trails being unsafe for lone travelers, freighters included, P. G. had raised his prices and was only sending out his freight wagons in caravans. I'd heard folks complain about his prices more than once, and the first time we tried to have some new tools freighted in, I understood why.

Murphy charged near as much to haul such things in as they were worth, and when we tried to find someone else to do the hauling, we couldn't. Simple as that.

We'd only been in Globe a couple of weeks when a Lieutenant Edmond Brice led a patrol of cavalry through town. He talked to Marshal Reynolds and then to each of us about the attack on the Smalley family. By that time Todd Smalley was able to describe a couple of the attackers, though Doc Jefferies asked me to stay real close to the boy while he did so.

Once he came to describing one man in particular, Lieutenant Brice knew right away who'd done it. The boy described the man who struck him as being big, with snow-white hair and a wicked scar around his neck.

Lieutenant Brice's face turned hard. "Hoag Willis," he said. "That description fits him like a glove."

Turned out Willis was already being sought by the army. He led a band of outlaws numbering anywhere from ten to twenty, and had drifted over from New Mexico some months earlier. He'd been raising hell ever since, ducking down across the border for a few months whenever things got too hot for him in Arizona.

For the first week and a half nobody stepped forward to take in Todd Smalley, so the boy stayed at Dr. Jefferies'. It seemed everybody knew the Smalleys, but no one knew if they had family elsewhere. Even the president of the small bank in Globe didn't know, and Trent Smalley had worked for him near three months.

I don't know how it was worked out legally, but finally a woman named Kate Crenshaw came forward and asked if she could give the boy a home. That's how it was done, and Todd went to live with her. She agreed with Doc Jefferies about me seeing the boy on a regular basis, so I went out to her place a couple of times a week.

Turned out she lived about two miles outside of Globe, and about four miles from the house we'd bought off Mathers. She'd had herself a husband once, but he'd ridden off for parts unknown some years earlier. Finally word came that he'd been killed.

Kate Crenshaw was in her mid-thirties and a fine-looking woman, though not one who pampered her looks. She was a working woman, and the toughness of her hands and dark tan of her face showed it. But there was a warmth to her smile, and a proud look in her eyes that made her almighty handsome.

She generally wore her hair up, but one morning when I rode out to her place to see the boy and she answered the door, her hair was down. It was red. Shimmering, copper red, and hung near to her waist. It was a fine sight.

She had a daughter named Laura, who was just sixteen. Laura was blonde, beautiful, and given to straddling a half-wild mustang and riding out across that lonesome country like nothing there would dare hurt her.

I reckon all three of us fell in love with Laura at first sight, though Billy was the only one serious about it.

Kate made a living, such as it was, by baking pies and cakes and such for Molly's, and anybody else who wanted them. She was saving in hopes of opening a bakery.

Kate took to making a regular thing of inviting the three of us over for Sunday dinner, and after tasting her pies and cakes, we weren't about to say no. Billy would have ridden five hundred miles just to see Laura, I reckon, and truth be told, I reckon I'd have ridden as far just to sit after dinner and hear a woman's voice. It was a pleasant, peaceful feeling after a hard day's work.

The one thing we'd all had our fill of was cattle, but horses and wild country were another story. We figured to eventually make a good part of our living by capturing wild mustangs and breaking them, and we all three loved to ride the wild country.

But it was Johnny who went exploring the most. Hunting wild horses wasn't safe at the time, but Johnny wanted to learn the country, and so he went off riding every chance he had. He kept off the skyline, watched his backtrail, and soon knew his way around the countryside pretty good.

Twice he had close calls despite his care, but each time he slipped away from trouble and made it back. On the second occasion he came riding back with a bullet burn across his leg, but it didn't seem to deter him none. A week later he was back out.

Then I figured it was my turn to get away and see some wild country. I'd been pretty much cooped up in town for six weeks, taking care of the smithy business and such, and something out yonder seemed to be calling to me.

I saddled up Shanghai, packed a week's worth of grub, turned the smithy over to Billy, and rode out, heading north. Billy had taken to the business of being a blacksmith like a duck to water, and I figured anything he couldn't yet handle could wait.

I went back up along the Verde River, turned west toward the Mogollon, and trotted my horse up to a bit of high country where I could take a good, long look around.

CHAPTER 4

FROM OUR RIDE along the Verde River, I'd known there was some pretty land out there, but I'd never in my life seen anything like the country that spread out before me. I'd come up out of the Verde Canyon, swung around and found a way up to the top of the Mogollon Plateau, and the expanse of country I saw took my breath away.

A good part of what I was looking at was Oak Creek Canyon, and at that time of year it was filled with color. From right where I stood, I could see blooming columbine, Indian paintbrush, and bluebells.

Here and there, lupine, poppies, beavertail, and sunflowers added their own splashes of color. I stood there for an hour or more, unable to tear my eyes away from the beauty.

Finally I rode off again, looking for something without really knowing what it was. And then, just like that, I found it.

Clear Creek started out up to the Little Colorado River some fifty or sixty miles northwest of where I sat my horse. It cut its way through the Mogollon, and eventually splashed into the Verde River. It was canyon country, high country, and country wild as any that God ever made.

Right there between the Mazatzal Mountains and the Mogollon Plateau, bordered on the north by Clear Creek and on the south by the Salt River, something reached inside me like a hand grasping me to the core. Without being able to put the why and wherefore into words that made any kind of sense, I knew that country was where I wanted to spend the remainder of my days. A man could run cows

29

in that country, but that wasn't so much what I had in my mind.

This was fine horse country, as well, and already had quite a few head running wild through it. But there was another reason I wanted to put roots down here, although I couldn't quite put it into words. I thought about it all the way back to Globe.

After what I'd seen out yonder, Globe had lost much of its shine. The town had been founded back in the early seventies on account of silver, or so I'd been told. Only, folks had discovered pretty soon there wasn't enough silver to keep the boom going.

However, there was plenty of copper. Before long, copper mining was the rule of the day, and copper mines (mostly huge, ugly, open pits) sprang up over a good part of southeast Arizona. Only a couple turned into long-running, big-money mines. A few of the smaller ones also hung on, and men still roamed the mountains, looking for new copper deposits.

According to the tales, there were some mighty rich gold deposits back in some of those Arizona mountains, as well as in the southeast. Whenever folks found a good bit of gold here and there, new legends of even richer deposits would abound. The deposits that were found, and the legends of others, had been bringing men into that country for years. If there was wealth of any kind to be had, be it gold, silver, or copper, many a man would brave Apaches, bandits, bad weather, and tales of haunted mines without a quiver.

Me, I didn't care about any of it. To my way of thinking, the beauty and wildness of that high country was in itself enough wealth for any man.

Wanting a bit more time to think things over, I'd camped a few miles north of Globe the night before, so when I broke camp and rode on in the next morning, it was still early when I arrived. The sun was up, and Globe was alive, but not by much.

There was nobody at the smithy, not that I expected there would be. While we sometimes slept there when the work piled up and we were late in finishing, most often we rode out yonder to the house. After giving Shanghai a good rubdown and a bait of corn, I walked on down to Molly's Restaurant.

Molly's was doing a booming breakfast business, and I had to wait fifteen minutes to get a table. Molly and the waitress she employed were hustling this way and that, carrying trays of food and big pots of coffee, but they both knew their business and got to me lickety-split.

Molly gave me a big smile and brought coffee without my needing to ask. "Let me guess," she said. "Four eggs sunnyside up, six slices of bacon fried crisp, four patties of sausage, and a stack of flapjacks? And keep the coffee coming?"

I returned her smile. "Yes, ma'am. That ought to do for starters."

Despite all the customers, Molly brought the food quicker'n scat, and I dug right in. Molly did some of the cooking herself, I knew, but somebody else back there in the kitchen did most of it. I'd no idea who it might be, but if it was a woman who looked half as good as she cooked, I'd like to meet her.

I'd heard it said more'n once that the way to a man's heart was through his stomach, and in my case there was cause to think it true. I liked my food, any food, and if it wasn't for all the hard work I put myself through I'd be fat as a bear.

Truth is, I was getting to the point in life when sitting around and getting fat didn't seem like such a bad idea. I couldn't think of many things more pleasing than to be a cranky, fat old man, sitting on the front porch in my rocker and griping at the world.

Especially if that rocker overlooked some of the country I'd seen on my ride.

By the time I was on the outside of that meal, even my

big appetite was satisfied. After paying for the meal and leaving a four-bit tip, I walked back down to the smithy. Billy was there by then, and was already pumping the bellows to heat up the forge.

"We were about to give up on you," he said. "Figured some Apache was riding about with your scalp on his war lance."

"Never saw sign of Apache, nor much of white man, for that matter."

"Did you make it up to the Mogollon like you planned on doing?"

"Yes, sir," I said. "I surely did."

That was all I said about it at the time, but it wouldn't stop gnawing at me. It was like some part of that country had seeped inside me while I was there, and now that I'd ridden out, my stomach and chest felt hollow.

Me and Billy put in a full day, and by dark we were more than ready to call it quits. Johnny had come riding in about noon, and while he was no hand at using a hammer and anvil, he more than made up for it by lifting and holding and carrying.

With the sun just a red ball sitting on the western horizon, we began closing down. What with our own horses and two more Johnny had bought, we had eleven horses out in the corral. We'd planned to run five of them out to the country place until we could add on more stalls, but hadn't gotten around to it.

Since the weather was fine, we left the horses in the corral and made sure the big trough was filled with water and there was enough hay thrown out for them. We generally kept our own horses in the stalls and pampered with more grain.

Truth is, one of the horses caught my eye. Johnny had just bought it off a farmer who was passing through Globe on the way to California. The horse was a big, spirited, palomino stallion, not a horse a cowhand would usually want unless it was gelded. Only I wasn't a cowhand, and if I had my druthers, I never would be again.

He was the kind of horse that would raise hell when out hunting horses as well . . . he'd probably catch wind of those wild mares and go running off to challenge the lead stallion for mating rights. But I didn't care. It ain't often a man sees a horse that he knows will get him out of trouble as quick as he can get himself in it, but I had the feeling that palomino was just such a horse.

Me and Johnny started dickering, and when all was said and done, I gave him two hundred for the palomino. Once the deal was closed, Johnny admitted he'd paid only fifty dollars for it.

"That farmer said the stallion would answer to the name of Nugget," Johnny said. "I ain't tried it yet."

"Hey, Nugget," I yelled. "Over here, boy."

Soon as I said his name, the palomino's head came up, his golden mane snapping the fading sunlight off like drops of red and gold water. Head high and tail raised, he trotted over to the rail fence.

"By God," Johnny said. "I thought I was putting something over on you, making that kind of profit, but I reckon I underpriced that horse."

"Yes, sir," I said. "You surely did. You ride him yet?"

"Ain't had need," Johnny said. "But he'll eat from a man's hand, so I 'spect he's saddle-broke. You gonna cut him?"

"Not a chance," I said. "We get us a keeping herd together, I might want to put him to stud."

"He'd make fine breeding stock, at that—By damn, Ben, I'm already regretting this deal."

"Not me. Reckon I'll ride him back out to the place when we go and see how he does with two hundred pounds astride his back."

"My guess is he'd carry more without a struggle. You planning to ride out this early?"

I grinned. "No, sir. I been out in those mountains a week or more . . . what day is this, anyway?"

"Saturday. Means we get Kate's apple pie tomorrow."

"You reckon it'll taste as good with a hangover? I got a terrible dry on."

Johnny laughed. "Not but one way to find out. Hey, Billy, come on and let's go. Ben's in a drinking frame of mind."

Billy was sitting inside the makeshift sleeping room. He had his britches off and was undoing the straps on his wooden leg. "You just hang on a minute," he said. "I got something chafing me."

Feeling down in the hollow where the stub of his leg went, Billy came out with a silver dollar. "I'll be damned," he said. "How do you suppose that got in there?"

"Likely got a hole in your pocket," Johnny said. "You're lucky that pegleg caught it for you."

Billy's face twisted up. "How many times I got to tell you, this ain't no pegleg. A pegleg ain't nothing but a sharp stick, and this thing is shaped proper."

Pulling the boot off the wooden leg, he held it up. "Just look at that," he said. "I put a bolt through the ankle so it could pivot when I step, and everything."

Johnny's eyes widened. "When did you do that?"

"Three, four days back. I saw it in a book over at Doc Jefferies'. See how this little block of wood keeps it from swinging down too far?"

"Does it work?"

"Sure makes walking look more natural. Don't have to stiff-leg it as much."

Billy pulled the boot back on the leg, strapped it on, pulled on his britches. He walked around a bit, and it did seem more natural. He still had a bit of a limp, but unless he wore his britches so tight you could see the ridge around his leg where he stuck the stump in, you'd never guess one of his legs was made of wood.

"Let's see how well you can walk on that thing with a gallon of whiskey in your gut," Johnny said.

"Lead on."

There were plenty of saloons in Globe, but our favorite was one most folks passing through didn't get to. It sat back down to the north so far it was near outside of town. A man named Dunie O'Brien owned the place, and in some ways it wasn't much.

The floor was covered with two inches of sawdust, and the last time the big mirror behind the bar had been broken, Dunie hadn't bothered buying another. Instead, he bought a painting somewheres, an overweight woman wearing only a feathered hat and a smile.

The food wasn't much to write home about. Dunie kept a big crock of pickled eggs on the counter, along with a platter of ham, cheese, and bread. These were free so long as you were buying drinks.

Most times, a big pot of chili simmered on a stove in the back, for folks who wanted hot food. And hot it was. Dunie made it himself, and tossed in the jalepeños with a shovel.

What O'Brien's did have going for it was the coffee, and the upstairs gals. The coffee was free, hot, and strong. And the upstairs gals were a cut above what most places had to offer.

Two of the women, Alice and Rhonda, Dunie had found right there in Globe. Alice claimed to be nineteen, had long, black hair, and a pert little face that was always smiling. Rhonda was tall, had chestnut hair, and a build that made men thump the floor and howl at the moon.

The other three women had been brought in from Denver. Fifi was no more than thirty, but had silver-gray hair that she claimed was natural. Lizzie was blonde, short, pretty as anything, and spoke with an accent that was pure South Carolina.

Joanie, now, was a mystery. She was cute as a button, friendly as a puppy, and willing to please, but about her past she wouldn't say a word. From her accent, I figured her to be southern, but now and again it faded off to being no accent at all, and I couldn't place it.

No matter. O'Brien's was a place where we felt comfortable, and that's what mattered most to any man without a place he could really call home. The girls he had working for him were pretty, friendly, and generally smelled sweet as mountain flowers, an unusual thing in itself.

Like most saloons, O'Brien's had a piano player, and the one banging out the tune when we walked in was named Levi Cranston. Me, I don't know enough about music to say how good he might have been, but he was loud and fast. That seemed enough to please most.

Dunie yelled out a hello to us when we came in, and we walked over to the bar. After getting a bottle of whiskey and a round of beer, we found a table and sat down. I went back to the bar and pulled three of the pickled eggs from the crock with a pair of tongs. I bit one in half on the way back to the table, then set the other two down next to my beer.

We drank for a time, until Alice sashayed over to the table. Johnny put his arm around her waist and pulled her down onto his lap. She ran a finger down his chest and gave him a big smile. "You coming upstairs?"

Johnny patted her bottom. "Reckon I am, at that," he said. He looked over at us. "You boys better rope a filly before the crowd comes in and corrals them all."

Billy leaned back and sipped his beer. "Guess I'll just sit here and drink," he said. "It's been a hard day."

Johnny winked at me. "It's that Laura Crenshaw," he said. "Man falls in love with a pretty young gal like that, he starts feeling like he ought to be true to her."

"Ah, go on," Billy said.

"Ain't saying there's anything wrong with it," Johnny said. "Just ain't the way my stick floats, is all. . . . What about you, Ben. You've had a shine for Joanie, and she'll sure be busy once those miners start pouring into town."

"Guess I'll sit here and drink a while myself," I said. "It has been a hard day."

Johnny shook his head. "Well, that's more for me," he said. Alice was a full-bodied woman, but Johnny stood up and trotted over and up the stairs with her in his arms. Halfway up he let out a war whoop.

Billy grinned, tossed down a whiskey, chased it with beer. "I'd not say it to just anyone," he said, "but I reckon Johnny wasn't far wrong. I never saw anything in my life prettier than Laura."

"You told her that?"

"No, sir. You think I oughta?"

I shrugged. "If you're looking for advice about women, you're asking the wrong buck. I never had much truck with any, outside of saloon girls."

"You do all right around Kate."

"Kate's different."

"Or maybe she's just different to you?"

"Might be? Like I said, I'm no hand."

Me an' Billy sat there and drank until standing up and walking a straight line was an iffy proposition. Johnny finally came back down and dropped into a chair. "Looks like I got some catching up to do."

Standing up, I caught the edge of the table to steady myself. "Time for me to call 'er quits," I said. "If I can get my horse saddled, I'm heading back out to the ranch."

"Never knew you to let off so early on a Saturday night," Johnny said. "Looks like your age is catching up with you."

"Can't outrun it forever."

Billy pulled himself to his feet. "Hang on, Ben. I might as well ride back with you."

Billy let out a big belch, and together we headed for the door. I don't have much memory of the ride out to the ranch, or of dropping into bed fully clothed when we arrived. I do recall the head-pounding hangover and queasy stomach that greeted me at first light.

CHAPTER 5

SITTING UP AND looking out the window, I saw that dawn was just easing its way onto the land but hadn't yet tugged the sun up over the horizon. Meager as it was, the light made my eyes ache, and started somebody inside my head beating on an anvil with a five-pound hammer.

My stomach got into the act then, trying its best to crawl out my throat. I fought it back down and went into the kitchen. There I built a fire in the cookstove and put a pot of coffee on.

While waiting for the coffee to perk, I went to the outhouse and took care of that chore. A rattlesnake slithered across my path and started to coil up as I stepped too close. Hooking the toe of my boot under its body, I sent it flying. It hit the ground ten feet away and crawled off.

It was a fine, cool morning, but too damn bright for the way I was feeling. Going back into the house, I went into the bedroom I'd picked, and dug out clean clothes and laid them on the kitchen table. I waited for the coffee to finish perking, then poured a big cupful.

Bundling up the clothes, my razor, and a bar of soap under my left arm, I picked up the coffee with my right hand and headed out the door. There was a fair trickle of a stream about a hundred yards from the house, and it was there I aimed.

The stream mostly was no more than fifteen feet wide and a couple of feet deep, but there was one wide, deep hole a ways east, and it was there we generally bathed. Stripping down, I took a deep breath and plunged in.

If the morning was cool, that crick water was cold! But,

39

by God, it felt good. With my hair dripping and my skin raising goosebumps, I eased over closer to the bank, picked up my coffee, and took a drink. I didn't lather myself up and rinse off until the last of the coffee was gone, and by then I felt like a new man.

Not that the hangover wasn't still with me. Only the blacksmith in my head was using a smaller hammer, and my stomach had decided it liked where it was and quit fighting me so hard. I shaved, dressed, and went back up to the house.

Billy was sitting at the table when I came in. He'd hopped out to the kitchen in his longjohns, not even bothering to strap on his leg. His hair was all a-swather, a stubble of beard covered his face, and his eyes were red as an October sunset.

"Ay, God," he said. "What got into you, Ben? Here the sun is barely up, an' you already had a bath."

"It was either that, or crawl off and die. If you feel half as bad as you look, I'd recommend the same."

"I'll get down to the crick by and by. We got any hair of the dog about?"

Going over to the cupboard, I took down a bottle of whiskey and passed it to Billy. He poured a generous dollop into his coffee, handed the bottle back. I filled my tin cup two thirds full of coffee and finished it off with two fingers of whiskey.

Sitting down and taking a long drink, I let out a sigh. "Now that hits the spot."

"I'll tell you the truth, Ben. I ain't so sure the drinking is worth the hangover."

"I've said the same thing myself a thousand times. Come the next trip into town, I always end up in some saloon, working on a brand new drunk."

After that cup of eighty-proof coffee, Billy felt better and went down for his own bath. I went out to the barn and checked on the horses. Least we'd had sense enough the night before to put them up proper. I turned both into the corral, pumped fresh water into the trough, and forked enough hay in to fill their bellies.

Johnny came riding in about ten, already bathed and clean shaven . . . and smelling to high heaven of some kind of rose water.

Sometime after noon, we started over for Kate's house and met her coming back from church. Todd jumped down from the wagon and ran to meet me. Scooping him up into my arms, I carried him into the house.

"I'm running late today," Kate said, "but I have dried apple pie and a rum cake I baked late last night. That should hold you until dinner."

We ate cake and pie, and washed it down with buttermilk while Kate fixed dinner. Then we ate dinner, finished off with more pie, and leaned back about to burst. Billy went off for a walk with Laura, Johnny played cowboys and Indians with Todd for a time, then thanked Kate for the meal, and rode back to our place.

Billy and Laura were still off somewhere, Todd was out playing in the yard, and I found myself alone with Kate. We got to talking, and next thing I know, I was telling her all about that country I'd seen out yonder, and how it made me feel.

Kate sat there in her blue and white Sunday dress, looking almighty handsome, and paying attention like my words meant something.

"They'll never fence in that land, Kate. Not in a hundred years, nor in a thousand. They'll never cut those mountains with barbed wire."

When I was finished she reached out her hand and touched mine. "If you feel so strongly about it, Ben, you should find a way to own that land.

"My husband was a dreamer, always planning one big

thing or another, but he never had the determination to make his dreams come true. I'd hate to see that happen to you."

After a time, I went out and played mumblety-peg with Todd. Billy and Laura finally came back, and with the sun setting low in the sky, me and Billy rode back home. We found a note on the table from Johnny, saying he was riding out to see if he could find some mustangs he'd come across a while back, and not to expect him back for a few days.

Most nights, if my back ain't hurting, I drop off to sleep soon as my head hits whatever I'm using for a pillow. That night I couldn't get to sleep for the life of me. Finally I got up and made coffee. Lighting a cigar, I went out onto the porch wearing only my longjohns, and sat there for a good two hours or more.

A full moon walked across a star-filled sky, and in the still of the night I listened to the sounds drifting in from the desertlike country to the south. A coyote howled, a rattlesnake buzzed, then a horse neighed long and loud.

Kate Crenshaw had set me to thinking in ways I never had before. It was true enough that I'd been looking for a place to spend out however many days I had left, but in my wildest dreams I'd not thought about such a wide, grandiose stretch of land.

Now I was thinking about it. There was no way of telling who owned that land out yonder until I checked with . . . who? There was a claims office in Globe, and the bank. One or the other ought to know. My hope was that a body could claim at least part of the land, but I just didn't know.

Come morning, though, I meant to find out. Come morning, I was going to see about buying myself as big a piece of heaven as any man on earth ever owned.

Going back inside, I eased into bed, and this time I fell right off to sleep.

Habits die hard, and like it or not, I was long since in

the habit of waking up before the sun. Lack of sleep or not, I did the same next morning. Wearing my longjohns and scratching my rear end, I opened the door and stepped out, planning on reaching the outhouse.

I hadn't taken more than three steps when a big Apache reared up from some brush and drew down on me with an old Henry repeater. By the time he squeezed the trigger, I was already running to get back inside. I heard the explosion of the rifle and felt the bullet buzz past my head at what seemed like the same moment.

As I dove headfirst through the door, a second bullet whizzed past me, struck the cookstove, ricocheted into a cupboard door. Something behind the door broke. A window shattered, then another. Scooting on all fours, I made my way to my rifle.

Billy appeared in the doorway, sleep and questions mixed in his eyes. A bullet came through the window and struck the door frame right next to his hand. He jerked away so fast he lost his balance and fell.

"Jesus H. Christ," he said. "What's going on?"

" 'Pache," I said. "Don't know how many."

"An' me without my leg on." He crawled off toward the back room, the trapdoor of his longjohns wide open. "Keep 'em busy while I get my leg on," he said.

Hustling over to a broken window, I peeked through. At first I didn't see a thing. Then the barn door flew open and a pair of Indians came running out, our horses in tow. Billy's horse jerked free and went running off. The other Apache jumped astride Nugget and kicked him with his heels.

I've seen horses buck, but I never saw one bow himself up like Nugget did. He went up in the air, lowered his head, and came down stiff-legged. When Nugget hit the ground, he stopped cold, but that Indian kept right on going. He landed right on top of his head and never moved a muscle.

Another Apache jumped from cover and ran toward him. Bringing my rifle up, I snapped off a shot. The Apache fell, then came up again and started running. I shot again, and this time he went down for keeps.

Billy had put on his leg and was at the other window with his rifle raised. A rabbit suddenly bolted from a clump of brush, and I levered three quick bullets through the area. Then silence settled in for good. Half an hour passed, then an hour. Through the brush we saw several Apaches ride off, apparently looking for easier prey. And it was only then that I realized that both Apache bodies were gone.

Rifles still at the ready, we moved outside. They were gone, all right, but from the blood left on the ground, the one I'd shot hadn't made it away by himself. Billy scouted around and found their trail while I gathered our horses.

By the time I found both, Billy was back. "They rode off to the south," he said, "but it looks like they came from over Kate's way."

A cold hand gripped my heart and squeezed. "Let's get saddled."

After seeing the way Nugget had bucked that Apache, I was more than a little leery about climbing in the saddle, but I needn't have been.

"It's the saddle," Billy said. "My guess is that horse has never been rode bareback. Looks like he don't care for it."

We stuck spurs to our horses and covered the ground between our place and Kate's at a gallop. Kate was all right, and so were Laura and Todd.

Laura met Billy at the door, threw her arms around his waist, and buried her face in his chest. Billy looked surprised, but I don't think he minded a bit.

"I was so frightened," Laura said. "All those Indians showed up, and Mom went outside and yelled at them. Then she brought them into the house!"

I guess my mouth dropped wide open, 'cause Kate told me to close it before the flies got in.

Kate flushed. "It does sound foolish now, but at the time I didn't know what else to do. They were trying to steal our horses, and I guess I lost my temper. I stepped outside, stomped my foot, and yelled at them to leave our horses alone. One of them raised a rifle, and I thought my heart would stop. Then another one stopped him, and they all walked over to me. I told them if they wanted something, they should ask for it.

"They stood there looking at me like I was crazy. So I told them I was about to fix breakfast, and I'd be glad to cook for them."

"You didn't?"

"She sure did," Laura said. "They came inside, and Mom cooked a ton of food. A couple of them spoke English, and talked to Todd and me. One of them touched my hair and said he had a wife named Ha-o-zinne, or something like that. He said my eyes reminded him of her."

"By God," Billy said. "Ain't that the name of Naiche's woman?"

"I think it is," I said. "I ain't certain, but I think it is."

"By God," Billy said again. "Naiche himself."

Coffee was perking on the stove, and when it stopped, Kate brought out the cups. We sat down at the table and sipped at the coffee while she finished her story.

"Laura didn't have the corner on being afraid," she said. "I was scared to death the whole time, but I did everything I could to keep them from seeing it."

"You did right," I said. "The Apache respects bravery above all else. If you'd shown fear, me an' Billy would likely be burying you about now."

Laura shivered. "That's an awful thing to say."

"The simple truth," I said. "Your ma saved your bacon,

and no two ways about it. How'd you get them to leave, Kate?"

She shrugged. "When they were through eating, they just left. The one Laura was talking about, did you say his name was Naiche? Anyway, he stopped at the door, looked at me, and laughed. He laughed all the way to his pony."

"My guess is he'd never had a woman yell at him, or invite him inside to eat his fill," I said. "I imagine it threw him for as big a loop as it did me."

Kate scrounged around and found enough food to fix us all breakfast. We ate, then Billy went out and hitched up her wagon so she could drive into town to buy more food. We rode in with her, me drivin' the rig, and Billy sittin' in the back with Laura and Todd.

We'd tied our horses behind the wagon, and Todd was struck by Nugget. "Seems to me you're old enough to have a pony of your own," I said. "If it's all right by Kate, I'll see what I can do about rounding one up."

Todd jumped up and leaned his head across Kate's shoulder. "Is it?" he asked. "Can I have a pony, Mom? Can I?"

"I guess so," she said. "But you'll have to rub it down and feed it yourself."

"I will. I promise!"

He dropped back down beside Laura and Billy, happy as a deer at a salt lick. Kate leaned over to me, tears in her eyes. "That's the first time he's called me Mom," she said.

Seeing how much this moved her really made a man think. Nobody had ever called me anything like Pa. The strange thing is, before now I'd never thought about it.

CHAPTER 6

ONCE IN TOWN, Billy said goodbye to Laura, then went on down to open the smithy, taking our horses with him. My hangover was gone as far as my headache and queasy stomach were concerned, but I still had the memory of it and figured I'd go a day or two without drinking.

That vow lasted as long as it took me to walk down to O'Brien's. He drew a beer as I stepped through the door, and it didn't seem proper to let it go to waste. While drinking, I talked to Dunie about the Apache attack, then about the land I'd seen out yonder.

"You want land out that way," he said, "it's likely you'll have to buy it. I hear there's already a couple of ranches in the area, though nobody's running many cattle yet.

"Another year or two, and that country will be overrun with beeves. Mark my word, lad. You want land up that way, you'd best buy it now."

Leaving O'Brien's, I checked at the claims office, figuring it a good place to start, since they also kept track of who owned what. It was, though the news wasn't to my liking. Near every acre of land in the area I wanted had been bought up, some of it by the bank.

I went to the bank to see if any of their land west of the Verde was for sale. I suppose you could say I got lucky there, though it was awfully expensive luck. Once I explained what it was I wanted, the fellow behind the window went into an office, then came back out. "Mr. Wilcox would like to speak to you about this," he said. "Right through the door there."

"Mr. Wilcox?"

47

"Yes, sir. He's president of this bank, sir. Right through the door."

Hat in hand, I walked over and stepped through the door. The office was well set up, with a fine rug and a big desk made of what looked to be mahogany. The man behind the desk was tall, and maybe sixty years old or better. But he was still a bull of a man, and his handshake was strong as any I'd felt in a time.

"You're Ben Hawkins?" he asked. "The man who brought Todd Smalley back to town?"

"Yes, sir," I said.

We sat down, and he closed the lid on an inkwell.

"Trent Smalley was a good man," he said. "He didn't work for me long, but I came to know him. It's ironic, but he was traveling in an effort to find work in a location where his family would be safer.

"His wife, Melissa, was terrified of this area. We tried to tell her that Globe was safe, but she wouldn't listen.

"Well, I guess there's nothing to be done about it now. I'm told you wish to buy some land, Mr. Hawkins?"

"Yes, sir," I said. "I expect I do."

Standing up, he took a large map from atop a file cabinet, unrolled it on his desk. "If you can point out approximately where the land in question is," he said, "I'll see if the bank can be of service."

Me, I'd learned to read a map back during the war, and it didn't take but a minute to find the Verde River, then to run my finger down to the valley between the Mazatzal Mountains and the Mogollon Plateau.

"That's it," I said. "I don't rightly know how much land I want, but I'd like it to sit so's I can have proper control of that valley."

Mr. Wilcox whistled. "I've never been out there," he said, "but I'm given to believe it's spectacular country. I know we either own or control quite a bit of land out there. Let me see . . ."

Mr. Wilcox dug into file cabinets, checked deeds, maps, and mortgages. Then he pulled out a big chart and compared it with the large map on his desk. Finally he sat down, leaned back, and looked at me.

"There's good news and bad news," he said. "The good news is that this bank can sell you some of the land you want." He ran his finger over the area I'd wanted. "There's about two hundred acres here by the Salt, just over a hundred lying against the Mogollons, and a bit more here by the Verde. If you'd like, I could arrange for you to file on that land at once. But the bad news is, it's all disconnected. Just about everything else is owned by either ranchers or miners who I'm certain would not sell at any price.

"But right here, starting a little farther north than what you wanted, but running down through most of that valley, the land is all for sale. There's just over forty thousand acres, and it's owned by a consortium in England. They bought it twelve or thirteen years ago, but they bought too soon. They've lost money on the land, and they want out.

"At the time they made the decision, this was the only bank in the area, so we signed a contract to sell the land for them on a commission basis. But they, unfortunately, set the terms."

"What are they?"

"They are asking forty-five thousand for the land, and I'm afraid the price is firm. They also forbid us to sell unless the prospective owner could pay twenty-five percent up front. That comes to eleven thousand, two hundred and fifty dollars, plus costs. Call it twelve thousand dollars."

It was a sum that took my breath away. When the three of us rode into the territory, we had a bit over three thousand between us, and never figured to ever again see so much money at one time.

A cowhand made from one to two dollars a day, and I'd known folks who ran prosperous stores and such who didn't turn more than eight or ten dollars profit a day. Twelve thousand dollars was as much as many a man made his whole life long. I said so to Mr. Wilcox.

He nodded. "Yes, Mr. Hawkins, it is a lot of money. But this is a growing land. I've seen miners who couldn't afford a beer walk in here after a big strike and hand me twenty thousand in gold.

"I wouldn't recommend putting your faith in striking gold, but there are other ways. Do you know P.G. Murphy?"

"I've seen him about."

"Well, there was a time only a couple of years back when he was dirt poor. Then he started his freighting outfit, and now he's one of the wealthiest men in this area. On paper, at least.

"Look, Mr. Hawkins, I respect what you've done for the Smalley boy, not only in rescuing him, but in the way you've watched over him since. We need men like you in this country.

"Unfortunately, the price of this land is out of my control, and so are the terms. But there is one thing I can do that may help somewhat. Can you raise two thousand in cash?"

I shook my head. "We've put about everything we have into fixing up the smithy, or our place out yonder. I might raise a thousand."

Mr. Wilcox drummed his fingers on the desk. "I'm afraid the stockholders wouldn't allow me to loan you the money for buying the land, and we can't loan money for a down payment on land we will probably hold the mortgage on.

"But what I can do is lend you up to three thousand against the mortgage on your smithy, and the land you hold outside of town."

"How would that help?"

He smiled. "It's simple, Mr. Hawkins. You would return two thousand to me, and I would use it to put a hold on the land you want. That I can do. Land is selling fast around here, but for two thousand, I can guarantee no one will buy the land out from under you for a period of four months.

"That might seem like very little time to raise twelve thousand dollars . . . ten thousand, actually. If you do buy the land, the two thousand will apply to the payment. I know four months isn't much time, but in this country anything is possible.

"If you could fill a hole, provide a service that people need, but don't have, or if you could find a way to provide a service they do have, but supply it cheaper than anyone else, you might raise a lot of money.

"But I'll be honest with you, Mr. Hawkins. The odds are you won't succeed and you'll break your back trying."

"What happens to the two thousand at the end of the four months if I don't come up with the ten thousand?"

"If you don't raise the rest of the money, you lose the two thousand, and you'll probably spend four or five years paying off your loan. Even if you do raise the needed capital, you'll have to take out a mortgage on the land, in addition to your current mortgages. And the payments on better than thirty thousand dollars won't be easy to make."

"It looks like a losing proposition all the way around," I said. "The kind of thing only a fool would try."

"It quite probably is, Mr. Hawkins."

Standing up, I stretched out my hand. "Guess I've always been a fool," I said, "but if my two partners will sign off on their shares, I reckon you got yourself a deal, Mr. Wilcox."

He smiled, shook my hand. "I'll have the papers drawn up at once. Come in day after tomorrow, and I'll let you sign your life away."

I walked out of the bank with my head swimming. The

sums of money we'd talked about were so big to my way of thinking that they didn't make sense. Maybe that's why I wasn't scared off. I just didn't know enough.

Walking down to the smithy, I found Billy pounding away at a piece of wrought iron. He asked what I'd been doing so long at the bank. Without putting any numbers to it, I told him I'd agreed to buy some land out yonder along the Verde.

His hammer was swinging in a regular pattern. "How much you paying for it?" he asked.

"What with interest, fees, and such truck, Mr. Wilcox said it ought to come to right at fifty thousand dollars."

Billy jerked so hard he missed the whole anvil on the downswing and near fell. He looked at me with pure shock all over his face. "Fifty . . . thousand . . . dollars? Ben, you done lost your mind! That's more money than . . . by Gawd, that's more money than I know how to figure."

"I reckon so. But I said I'd do it. Why don't you close down shop and we'll go talk about it over a beer."

"Beer, hell. It'll take whiskey to make sense of that much money."

"It might at that," I said. "It might at that."

Closing down the smithy, we walked down to O'Brien's and ordered a bottle.

We took to pouring shots of whiskey, and chasing them down with beer. It wasn't long before we were starting to slur our words a bit. A few more drinks and we stopped caring about money, land, or anything else.

It was fairly early yet, but now and again some miner or cowhand would drift in. P. G. Murphy came in along about four, wearin' a suit that must have cost more'n we made at the smithy in a month.

"You are now looking at the last freighter in this whole damned part of southeastern Arizona," he said. "The drinks are on me."

A few cheers went up, but what he said put a whole new

idea in my head. It had to work a bit to get through the fog, but it made it in somehow. Dunie O'Brien was busy pouring drinks for those that stampeded to the bar, but we still had a bit of whiskey left, and I poured myself a glass, spilling about half on the table.

It wasn't what he said that bothered me so much as the high and mighty way he said it. That, and just looking at the way he dressed and strutted around. Without thinking, I stood up and hoisted my glass.

"No, sir," I shouted. Murphy turned to look my way, as did most of those drinking. "No, sir," I shouted again. "Might be you got the only freight outfit today, but by God, it won't be by itself for long.

"Here's to Ben Hawkins, Billy Martin, and Johnny Stevens, the best damned freighters in the territory."

Murphy looked at me, surprise plain on his face. "You're the blacksmith, aren't you?"

I nodded, and he smiled. "I wasn't aware that you also ran a freight line," he said.

"Don't," I said. "Not yet. But we will."

Taking half a step forward, my toe caught on the table leg. What with all the whiskey in me, that was just enough to trip me up. I staggered a couple of steps, then fell facedown. The last thing I remember hearing before passing out was the sound of P. G. Murphy laughing.

When I woke up it was pitch dark. After a time I realized I was in the sleeping room at the smithy. About then my stomach started heaving, and I dashed for the door, my head spinnin' like a top. I made 'er out back before emptying my stomach, but not by much.

Going back inside, I staggered back to that little room, dropped down on the cot, and didn't stir again until first light. That little room had a window to match, but it was pointed due east, and when light came trickling in, it was enough to wake me.

That little man with the hammer was back, and this time

he had a friend with a couple of hot pokers who was doing his best to stick them through my eyes from the inside out. Sitting up, I fumbled for a cigar, found one, struck a match. My hand was shaking so bad it took three tries to make the flame and the cigar meet up.

Memory came flooding back, and none of it was pretty nor pleasant. "Damn my soul," I said aloud. "I reckon God never made a bigger fool."

Nobody jumped out to argue the point.

For the first time I saw that Billy was lying on the other bunk, sprawled in his clothes. He snorted, rolled over, but didn't awaken.

Going out into the main part of the smithy, I looked around. The work was starting to pile up. Going out back, I dipped my head into the water trough, and then sat on the edge, letting the water drain from my hair down my shirt collar. I took a long draw on the cigar, then dropped it in the mud and ground it out with my boot.

Walking back inside, I started moving tools around, figuring to get things ready for work if I lived through the morning. I tossed a long piece of iron over onto a bench, and it clanged around a good bit in landing.

"Hell's bells," somebody yelled. "Who's making all that damned racket at this hour?"

The voice came from the small loft back behind me. Looking that way I saw a head pop into view. It was covered with a mop of gray hair, and had a face that looked to have outlived half a dozen bodies.

"I'm making it," I said. "Who the hell's asking?"

The man sat up, twisted around, and came down the ladder. He was five inches or so under my height, and likely didn't weigh much over one-forty. On the other hand, while he'd been uncommonly hard on his face, I figured he wasn't near as old as I'd first taken him to be.

"Name's Darby Sullivan," he said. "Me and that young

fellow drug you over here last night after you passed out. Didn't figure you'd mind me sleeping up yonder."

"No, I reckon not. I'm beholden to you."

"Not as much as you're gonna be," he said. "If you wasn't just flapping your gums to hear the sound of your own voice last night, I'm the man you need to start up a proper freighting outfit."

I'd forgotten all about that, but once Sullivan brought it up, that memory rushed back in to join the others. "I reckon I must've been drunk or outta my mind," I said, "but when Murphy said he had the only freight outfit in this part of Arizona, it seemed like he could stand some competition."

"Old P.G. ain't the kind to stand for nothing. But the right man could sure make money hand over fist by hauling freight right now . . . if he didn't go under in the doing."

My mouth felt like it had been stuffed full of cotton, and my head throbbed. "Let me get cleaned up a mite," I said, "and we'll talk about it. I don't know about food, but I'd sell my soul for a gallon of hot coffee."

Digging my shaving kit and a reasonably clean shirt from my saddlebags, I went out back again. Stripping to the waist, I washed and shaved, then let the water out of the horse trough, and pumped fresh in.

When I walked back in, Billy was standing there jawing with Sullivan. "Let's go," I said. "Daylight's a-wasting."

Billy looked like death warmed over. "Where we headed?"

"To hell," I said, "sure as anything. But I ain't going without my fill of coffee."

Once at the restaurant, I ordered coffee, and told Sullivan to get whatever he wanted. He ordered eggs, sausage, biscuits, and gravy. I'd not thought my stomach would handle food, but once he took to eating, I figured I'd give it a try. I ordered, and it didn't set as bad as I'd thought it would.

Waiting until Sullivan was finished eating, I took a long drink of coffee. "If you got a horse to show me," I said, "you might as well trot him out where I can see how he prances."

Sullivan rolled a cigarette and lit it. "I got a horse," he said. "I got the prancin'est, prettiest horse you ever saw, if'n you're the man to ride it."

"Tell us about it."

Blowing out smoke, he started talking.

CHAPTER 7

DARBY SULLIVAN STARTED talking, telling us about P. G. Murphy's outfit primarily, and he knew plenty. He told us how many wagons Murphy ran, how much he charged, and who his main customers were. He told us places Murphy wouldn't send his wagons, and how much he jacked up prices to folks in other areas.

Me and Billy sat there listening, and I had to admit, Sullivan made the whole thing seem like a Sunday walk.

"How do you know so much about Murphy's freight line?" I asked.

Sullivan snorted. "Worked for him since the day he came into Arizona."

"You don't work for him now?"

Sullivan looked like he wanted to spit. "Hell no, I don't work for him. The son of a bitch fired me about six weeks back."

"What for?" Billy asked.

"Stealing, was the way he labeled it."

I sipped my coffee. "Did you do it?"

Sullivan stubbed out his cigarette and started rolling a second. "I did what he claimed. Only I sure as hell didn't consider it stealing.

"One of the boys told me Murphy wanted to see me, so I went over to his office. He weren't there, an' I settled down to wait. After a time, I noticed this bottle of whiskey sitting on a shelf.

"Well, sir, I'd just come in off a ten-day freight run, and I had a terrible dry on. Figuring Murphy wouldn't mind, I found a glass and poured myself about four fingers of the stuff. He came in, looked at that whiskey in my hand, and threw a holy fit.

"He claimed to have brought that stuff in all the way from Scotland, or some such place. Said he paid near fifty dollars for that one little bottle. Son of a bitch said I was a no-good thief and fired me on the spot."

"That don't hardly seem right," Billy said. "What kind of fool would pay fifty dollars for a bottle of whiskey, anyway?"

"The thing is, Murphy never thought twice about grabbing up one of our bottles without asking," Sullivan said. "Many's the time he'd reach under the seat and haul out a bottle, and we never complained. I sure never thought the bastard would fire me for taking a drink of *his* whiskey. Course, I didn't know he was paying fifty dollars a bottle for it, neither."

"You really think a man could take enough business away from Murphy to make starting up a freighting outfit pay off?" I asked.

"I should smile! Murphy's got every customer for fifty miles around madder than a rattlesnake in the blind. He's charging three, four times the going rate, and making a lot of folks pick up their loads thirty miles from nowheres.

"Of course, part of it ain't Murphy's fault. There's been so many wagons robbed, and skinners shot, or shot at, that finding good men who'll work at a fair rate is near impossible. And won't nobody run a lone wagon. Murphy never sends out less than four wagons, and runs whole damned caravans whenever he can. He makes folks wait for their freight until he gets enough orders to run a whole string of wagons, and if some outlying miner or rancher wants a load, the best Murphy will do is deliver it to the closest town. So I'd say there'd be plenty of folks lining up to have their freight hauled by a fair outfit."

"If there's so much money to be made," Billy asked, "then why ain't somebody tried to go against Murphy?"

"They have," Sullivan said. "Three times, that I know about. None of them lasted long enough to matter. One fellow got himself shot to doll rags on his first run, and another went broke because he had so many wagons wrecked and so much freight ruined—"

"Who done that?" I asked.

Sullivan shrugged. "Some say outlaws, an' some say Indians. And while they don't say it very loud, there's some say Murphy himself paid to have it done. Me, I don't know. I'd not put it past him to have a wagon wrecked, or a skinner roughed up. But I don't know as he'd have a man shot. Don't know as he wouldn't, either."

"You said you knew of three people," Billy said. "What happened to the other one?"

Sullivan swore. "What was it you think Murphy was celebratin' last night? The last fellow up agin him was a Missourian named Jobe Richardson. Anyways, Richardson was running his outfit from just outside of Tucson, so I rode down there last week looking for work after Murphy fired me. His widow told me that somehow or another, Jobe got hisself run over by his own wagon a couple of weeks back. Then the skinner driving the other wagon up and quit cold. She said the next day Murphy showed up and offered to buy all the wagons and mules, but the price he offered wasn't a tenth of what it all was worth. She said she told Murphy what he could do with his offer."

Molly came over and poured me a fresh cup of coffee, and I sipped at it. "How much would it take to start up a proper outfit?"

"A man could get a running start with two big wagons and a couple of trailers. If he wasn't afeared to make lone runs into those areas that Murphy won't send his wagons to, he wouldn't even have to cut prices much below Murphy's, either.

"Puttin' a dollar figure on it, now—that's a hard thing. I reckon you got enough room there at the smithy to run mules in a corral and set up your wagons. Might have to build on a little office, but that wouldn't be much.

"They's wagons a-plenty to be had, though many could stand fixing up. Mules are another story. They can be had, and they ain't as costly as good horses, but you'd need a whole damned herd.

"You want to run proper wagons, conestogas, or Pittsburghs, as some call them, you need a bunch of mules. I've seen men run as many as twenty mules on a team, but you sure don't need that many.

"But if you want to haul enough freight to matter, you need a trailer behind your Pittsburgh, and then you beter have ten or twelve mules. In this country you might want to add an extra pair just in case you lose a couple.

"Now, if'n you buy mules by the herd, you can get 'em for something less than a hundred each, but that still figures up to be real money."

"Just give us a cash dollar figure."

"All right. Let's see. For two wagons, two trailers, and fifty mules? Generally I'd say right around five thousand dollars. But it just so happens I know where you can get yourself ever' bit of that for exactly half the price. For twenty-five hundred, you can have a whole damned outfit that's waiting to go. One of the wagons needs a good bit of work, but nothing you can't take care of right there in the smithy."

"How do you know about such things for sale?"

"Missus Richardson asked me if I could find a buyer."

"She the one that set the twenty-five-hundred price?"

"We come up with it together."

"What's in it for you?"

Sullivan scratched his chin. "A bit, I reckon. Ten percent of whatever she gets, if you got to know. And if you be the one that buys, I'd want a job. I can skin or swamp, I know ever' one of Murphy's customers, and I know the freighting business from the ground up."

I sat there a minute, staring off into space. Finally, I looked at Billy then back at Sullivan. "Give us some time to think it over, and we'll let you know."

"Don't take too long. That's more'n a fair price."

"We just need a little time. How can we find you?"

Sullivan raised and lowered his bony shoulders. "Been camping outside of town for the last week. Down yonder there by the crick. 'Spect you can find me there most anytime, less I'm out hunting or such."

"Good enough. Tell you what—if you ain't heard from me by day after tomorrow, you can figure I ain't interested."

Sullivan bobbed his head. "I guess that ain't askin' too much time. But don't take no longer than that, else I'm going to ride over to Phoenix and see if I can sell the widder's property there. Only reason I thought to try Globe first was on account of Murphy. It'd sure please me to see a freighting outfit start up right under his nose."

"We'll let you know."

Sullivan finished off his coffee, stood up. "I'll stay as close to camp as I can until I hear from you," he said.

After he left I wiped my mouth. "Best we get the smithy open," I said, deliberately avoiding the subject of freighting. "Else we're gonna get so backed up we'll still be working come midnight."

"Might sweat out some of this hangover," Billy said. "My pa always said hard work was the best cure."

We walked down to the smithy, only to find two men waiting for us. One man's wagon needed a new tongue, and the other's wagon had a wheel that was about to give way. Two of the spokes were busted, but I figured I could salvage the wheel with some work.

Backed up with work as we were, getting to those jobs the same day wasn't likely, and I said as much. Neither man seemed to mind, so I told 'em to leave the wagons and I'd fix them soon as I could.

Both men walked off and I saw them go in the nearest saloon. Me and Billy got to work. And work we did. We had two big anvils, and in two shakes we were pounding iron on both. There's a rhythm to such work that lets off the need to think much about what you're doing, and pretty soon my mind was out yonder, taking in the wide Mogollon Plateau.

That's one of the things I always fancied about blacksmithing work. You bring the hammer down hard on a piece of hot iron, and the loud ring of it sings out for a hundred yards. Then you let the hammer bounce over onto the anvil to take out the vibration and get control again. If you're swinging right, the hammer should give three little bounces on the anvil, and then you swing it again.

Without even meaning to, me and Billy fell into a pattern, first his hammer ringing and then mine, and a pretty sound it was. We moved from one job to another without the need to speak, and I just let my mind wander where it would.

I sure enough wanted that land out yonder. I'd never seen a spot half as pretty. It would be fine to run some horses on that land—hell, maybe even some cattle, so long as I didn't have to drive them up the trail.

I was tired of riding from one ranch to another in search of work, and of winding up every month with no money in my pockets and nothing but more age to say the time had passed.

I'd figured a smithy of my own would handle such feelings, and it did, to a point. Only swinging a hammer and working with hot iron ain't a job that sits well with age. Might be I could go at it for another ten or fifteen years, but where'd I be then?

The truth is, I never minded hard work. Liked it, in fact. But I was smart enough to know there comes a time when the body needs more rest than a dirt-poor working man can give it.

And while I'd not say it out loud, I was wondering what kind of mark I was going to leave behind, and who'd be there to take up where I left off.

I had nobody who'd care a lick if I dropped dead tomorrow. Might be Billy and Johnny would miss me for a time, but I figured that would be it.

But as much as I wanted that land, everything was all getting complicated. Fifty thousand dollars was just fool talk. Yet, here I was about to mortgage the smithy and the old Mathers place out yonder, and talking about starting a freight outfit. All that from standing atop a big hunk of rock and looking down into a valley!

It was all getting to be too much. I wanted a drink . . . I wanted a three-day drunk, truth be told. I wanted to get good and drunk, and spend a week's wages on one of the whores down at O'Brien's.

If it hadn't been for P. G. Murphy, and Kate Crenshaw, I might've done just that and said to hell with everything else. It was Murphy that struck the first blow.

Way we were workin' and the way my mind was runnin' hither and yon, the time flew. Next thing I knew Billy was shouting at me that it was well past lunch.

I looked over at Billy; he stood there sweating to beat the band. He took off his leather apron and his shirt was soaked front and back, and his bare arms shone with the wetness.

"I figure it's near two o'clock," he said. "I could sure use a bite to eat and something to wash it down."

Glancing up the street, I saw the shadows were beginning to stretch a bit. I took off my own apron. "I'd have swore it wasn't near noon yet," I said. "How's your hangover?"

"Guess my pa was right. I sweated it out, along with enough water to make a fair-size river."

"Then let's go get something to eat," I said. "I guess a beer wouldn't hurt none, neither."

We walked down to O'Brien's, ordered a beer, and made

sandwiches from the ham platter. We each took three pickled eggs and found a table. I'd no more than taken my first swig of beer and bitten into a pickled egg when I'll be damned if P. G. Murphy didn't walk through the door. His eyes lit on me and he grinned from ear to ear.

"Hey, muleskinner," he yelled. "I walked past that little smithy of yours this morning. Funny, but I didn't see a single wagon or even an old mule. Guess they're all out making freight runs?"

The temptation was strong to get up and see if I could stomp his gizzard out. Instead I made myself grin in return. "No, sir," I said. "We won't close the deal on the wagons and mules for a week or so yet. But along about the end of next week, you come by and I'll show you wagons and mules."

Something in my voice must have convinced him I meant what I said. He opened his mouth, closed it without speaking, then walked over to the bar and talked to Dunie for a few minutes. Then he turned around abruptly and started toward the door. He glanced my way and said, "If you're serious about starting your own freighting outfit, you'd do well to reconsider. I don't like people who try to take what's mine."

I sipped my beer. "You can always sell out," I said. "I'll give you a fair price."

His face reddened. "You'll give me—by God, you have a nerve! I spend more on clothes in a month than you're worth."

"Bet you spend plenty on whiskey, too. Why, I bet a man like you might spend as much as fifty dollars on a single bottle."

"How in hell did you know—Do yourself a favor, blacksmith. Stick to making horseshoes. You get in my way and I'll run you over."

With that, Murphy stormed on out. Dunie brought over three beers, sat one in front of me, one in front of Billy, and swigged from the third. He sat down and leaned thick forearms on the table. "These are on the house," he said. "I've been waiting for someone to tell Murphy where to get off. Were you serious about starting a freight outfit of your own?"

The truth is, I still had a bit of doubt. "It ain't certain yet," I said. "I know someone wanting to sell, though. A lot of it depends on the price."

"I'd like to see it," Dunie said.

"What was Murphy jawing at you about?"

Dunie shrugged. "He's been wanting to buy me out, but I'm not wanting to sell. I might, if the price was right, but the way it looks, Murphy must be short on cash money. Might be he's just being tightfisted, but he's wanting to pay for the place a little at a time."

"Low on cash? The way I hear it, he's one of the wealthiest men in these parts."

Dunie took a drink of his beer, wiped foam away from his big mustache. "Probably is. But he's expanded his business awfully fast, and I hear he's bought into several mining operations that didn't pan out. Lost a mint, the way I hear it. Anyway, if you go up against him, you watch yourself. Murphy ain't the kind to take losing easy."

"I'll keep it in mind."

Dunie went back to the bar. We finished eating, then walked back to the smithy. By the time we closed down it was dark. We rode back out to the ranch, with me still thinking about what to do and how to do it.

Next morning, I let Billy ride into town alone, while I rode over to check on Kate. If I had any doubts left, she put them to rest quick.

CHAPTER 8

KATE HAD HER hair down again, and looked mighty fetching. Todd ran over and jumped onto my lap while Kate fixed breakfast. He asked me about the pony I'd promised him. I'd been so busy I'd not yet given it much thought.

"I'm looking about," I said. "We got to get the exact right one, and such a good pony ain't easy to find."

He looked disappointed.

"Don't worry, boy," I said. "We'll find one. Tell you what. I heard of a rancher up north a ways, and folks say he's got some fine ponies. I'll ride up there next week and see if I can find you a real grasscropper."

That cheered him up, and he slid from my lap. Laura came out from somewheres then, sleep still heavy in her eyes. I had to admit, even half asleep, she was prettier than most women after they were all fixed up. Billy was sure taken with her, but I reckon he had lots of competition. Kate was trying to hold back on men riding out to see Laura, but all the girl had to do was come to town and cowhands and miners alike poured out just to see her. And I didn't blame them a bit.

The only thing about it was Billy. He was young, but he'd already ridden some hard roads, and while he wasn't much on letting out his feelings to me and Johnny, it seemed to me that he'd already wrapped a lot of his dreams around Laura Crenshaw.

It was my experience that grabbing hold of a dream was a lot like grabbing a rattlesnake . . . get the right grip and everything was fine, get the wrong one and you'd likely get bitten good.

I hoped Billy had the right grip so's his dreams didn't swing around and bite him.

I told Kate about the run-in I'd had with P. G. Murphy, and she made a harumphing sound. "I've met Mr. Murphy," she said. "He may portray himself as a gentleman, but he isn't one.

"Back when he first came to Globe, he decided a woman with no husband and a child to raise should be happy to receive his attentions. Well, I might have been, had Mr. Murphy approached me in a proper way. He didn't. What he wanted he could have found at any saloon in Globe."

"Might be he ain't no gentleman," I said, "but he sure owns a bunch of wagons, and he's got a flock of men working for him. And from what I hear, he's reputed to be a tough man, to boot. Besides, I don't 'spect I can lay claim to being a gentleman myself."

Kate put her hands on her hips and gave me a look that could've curled paint. "Ben Hawkins," she said, "don't you dare say such a thing. I've known you for two months now. You've been inside my home on many occasions, and I've been alone with you more than once. You have never behaved as anything other than a gentleman.

"If my opinion means anything, being a gentleman has nothing to do with wearing expensive suits or using fine words. Being a gentleman comes from how you treat other people, pure and simple."

That flustered me. I'd been called a lot of things in my life, but most of them couldn't be repeated in mixed company. "Gentleman" hadn't appeared nowhere on the list until now.

"And another thing," she said. "When Mr. Murphy rode into Globe, he wasn't wearing expensive suits, and he didn't own a big freighting company. And nothing I can think of would please me so much as seeing him leave Globe the same way he came in.

"I think you should start your own freighting line, Ben.

Not because I'd like to see Mr. Murphy get his comeuppance, but because I want to see you make your own dreams come true."

Well, sir, I sat there for a spell not knowing what to say. Then I sipped at my coffee. "Yes, ma'am," I said at last. "If I can get those mules and wagons, I guess I'll do just that."

Once I'd eaten, I rode back into Globe and started working at the smithy with Billy. Johnny came riding in that evening, looking like he'd been through hell again. He didn't know a thing about the fifty thousand I'd agreed to pay for the land, nor about mortgaging the smithy and the land Mathers had sold us.

We sat down for a powwow at O'Brien's that evening, and I laid it all out for him. Then I said, "The thing is, if you both agree, I want all three of our names on that land out there. There's sure plenty to go around."

"I'm all for it," Billy said. "I'm tired of being near broke, and I'm tired of looking up to others. We get ourselves that land out there, and we won't have to walk behind no man."

"Don't have to now," Johnny said to Billy. "But I can see what you're thinking. You own yourself a third of that land, run a bunch of horses, maybe even some cattle, and that Laura Crenshaw would sure enough think you're a good catch."

Billy's face reddened. "I can't say I ain't thought of that," he said. "A girl like that, well, she could have her pick of men. I just can't think of no reason why she'd want me. All I got is a wooden leg and what I make at the smithy."

"You got a lot more than that," Johnny said. "But I reckon you can count me in on the deal, with a couple of provisions."

"Name them."

Johnny took a long drink of beer, rolled a cigarette, struck a match, and lit the cigarette. "You know I ain't much on workin' at a smithy," he said. "Don't know how I'll make out as a muleskinner, either, though I'm willing to do what needs done. But I got another way of looking at this. If it don't make sense to you, just say so."

"Go on and say it."

Johnny leaned forward. "Seems to me we stand a better chance of making the down payment if we don't throw all our eggs in one basket. We each got our strengths, and we ought to play on them. I'll drive one of those wagons, if somebody can show me how to handle twenty mules, and I'll sure put in for paying my share. But I want time away to go yondering.

"I've been scouting this country far and wide, Ben. Once you get out away from the trails, you just wouldn't believe how wild it gets. Wild, dangerous, and full of mustangs.

"I've been watching three different herds, and in time I figure to get them all. But I think I can get near one full herd . . . must be fifty, sixty horses, with not but a little work."

"How's that?" I asked.

Johnny blew a cloud of blue smoke. "I saw that herd spooked three times. Once a cougar grabbed itself a colt, another time a couple of Apaches went after them, and the third time I spooked them myself. All three times they done the same thing."

Johnny took out the stub of a pencil, and a little tally book. He drew a small map, made a big circle on the map, placed a small circle inside that. Then he stuck the point of his pencil on the big circle. "This here's the country about twenty, thirty miles the other side of the Santa Cruz. This tiny little circle is a draw.

"Now, that's a funny little draw," he said. "It's too danged small to call a canyon, but it's way the hell too steep and rocky for a horse to make it up the sides. Once in there, the only way out for a horse is to go out one end or the other.

"Thing is, every time that herd of mustangs is spooked, they run right through that little draw to make their getaway."

"How's that help you catch them?" Billy asked.

"That little draw ain't more than thirty-five, forty yards wide at the one end, and no more than twenty yards at the other. I figure to go out there and build enough fence sections to block off both ends of that draw. I figure it'll take a couple of weeks or so to do it right. Then, come morning, I'll wait till that herd is through, then close off the wide end. Then I'll spook the herd, and once they're inside the draw, I'll block off the other end."

I whistled. "It sounds like more work than a man ought to try. You'll need help."

Johnny nodded. "Some. But that's wild country, and I can't go riding in there with a bunch of men. What I figure to do is sneak in and build the fence sections alone. That way I can stay out of sight better.

"Then, when everything is ready to go, I'll ride out, hire myself a man or two, and go back. We'll trap the herd, cull out the poor stock, and drive the rest back to town. Phoenix, maybe. Depends how things go.

"I figure if everything goes right, I ought to be able to bring back thirty-five, maybe forty head. Even for unbroke stock, that adds up to real money. If I take time to break them, I ought to put near three thousand dollars in my pocket."

"That's fine by me," I said. "It don't matter to me how we raise the ten thosand, just so we do. Might be you can scout out some freighting jobs for us in your riding. It'll take time for word of us to get around."

"That I can do. And there's something else."

"Sure."

"I know how you feel about cattle, Ben, only I'd sure like to run some up yonder, should we get that land."

"I guess I would, too," I said. "I've been thinkin' it over, and it ain't cattle I don't like, it's pushing another man's beeves up the trail."

"Hell, the really long drives are pretty much over, anyway," Johnny said. "The railroad is spreading out so fast that pretty soon a man won't be able to take a long walk without tripping on one.

"But those being the conditions, I'm in. If I can't raise my share of the money, I won't complain about walking away."

"There won't be any walking away no matter how we raise the money," I said. "If we're all in this, then it's all the way, no matter who puts in the most. Besides, it sure looks like we're going to need to hire a couple of men, no matter how we go about it. 'Specially since either me or Billy will have to be at the smithy a good part of the time.

"And it just makes sense. Between those wild mustangs, the smithy, and hauling freight, we'll have money coming in from three sides. I still don't know as it's going to be near enough, but at least we'll have a shot."

"Where does Murphy get his smithy work done?" Johnny asked. "Seems like he'd need plenty, what with all those wagons and mules he owns."

"He's got his own blacksmith down at the freight yard. They don't do anything for the general folks, but I guess it's enough to handle what work he needs."

"That's about what I figured," Johnny said. "Only I was hoping you and Billy were doing at least some of it. That'd make Murphy less likely to put us out of business in any kind of permanent way."

"No such luck," Billy said.

Johnny finished his beer and stood up. He was still cold sober, but his eyes had a faraway look. "I'm all for this, Ben. I mean it. I want me some land to call my own, and I want some horses and cattle to run on it.

"Only I ain't sure I'm done yondering yet. I stay in town for a couple of days, and it feels like my innards are gonna explode. I get to looking out toward the horizon and wondering what lies on the other side.

"It's funny sounding, maybe, but sometimes I feel like

there's something or someone out there calling to me. I don't rightly know what or who it is, but it keeps on calling, and pretty soon I got to ride out and see if I can find it.

"Never have. Maybe I never will. Or maybe that land out there by the Mogollon is it. I don't know, Ben. I just don't know.

"Well, reckon I'll take myself a nice long walk, then turn in early. See you galoots come morning."

Johnny walked on out, and for a minute neither of us said a word. "Never knew Johnny to call it quits so early," Billy said. "What do you suppose he meant by all that talk?"

"Just got the urge to see the elephant," I said. "Likely that's all it is."

"My pa used to say that. Never did really know what it meant."

"Just means a man gets the urge to see things he never saw before. Guess I've felt the same way myself a time or two."

That's all I said to Billy, but I figured there was more to it than just the urge to see new things. Johnny was still young by most standards, but old enough to feel the years slipping past. And far as I knew, he didn't have much in the way of family, and he'd never mentioned a woman in all the time I knew him.

"A free-riding man gets lonely," I said. "He sure enough does."

I said the words softly, not even meaning to say them at all. Billy raised his eyebrows. "Huh, what'd you say, Ben?"

"Nothing. Just thinking out loud."

"Don't know why," Billy said, "but somehow Johnny put me in the dumps."

"You're getting the big lonesomes yourself. Drink another beer and cut out the gal you like best, and you'll be your old self again."

Billy shook his head. "Don't guess I will." He stood up.

"Guess I'll ride out to the ranch myself." He started for the door, stopped, looked back at me. "Ben?"

"Yeah?"

"You really think Laura would go for me . . . if I was part owner of a big spread like we're planning, I mean?"

"She'd be a fool if she didn't," I said. "Big ranch or no."

Billy looked at me for several seconds, then nodded his head and went on out.

But damned if the big lonesomes didn't sneak up and bite onto my leg then. I sat there trying to shake them off, but it was no use. Then Joanie came over and sat down. She touched my hand and looked at me out of those pretty green eyes.

"You look like your best girl just ran off with a traveling man," she said.

"It'll pass."

"Why don't you come upstairs," Joanie said, "and I'll see if I can push it along?"

For the first time all evening, I smiled. "Why not?" I said. "Why the hell not?"

Still holding my hand, Joanie led me upstairs to her room. I don't know as she ran the big lonesomes all the way off, but she sure made them let go of my leg.

CHAPTER 9

IT'S ALWAYS BEEN a funny thing to me how time flies past when something bad is headed your way, and how it crawls along like a crippled snail when you're anxious to get moving on to something you want to do. Me, I never was the kind to worry about things. Maybe because I never had time to worry, nor enough money to make worrying a needful thing.

Hard work was always a thing I liked. Only as I got older the work just kept getting harder and harder, and my back started hurting on a regular basis. Some mornings I'd wake up with my whole spine stiff as a frozen snake, and my hands numb and aching.

Mostly it came from pushing other men's cattle up the trail, from sleeping and working in the rain and the cold, and from time piling years on my body the way a man piles gear on a jackass. It was along about then that I started looking for a place to light, where I might sleep in a soft bed, spend time on my front porch soaking in the warm sun, and not have to spend long days in the rain and cold less'n I wanted.

Now, of a sudden, I was trying to buy what seemed to me about half the land God ever made. And it was starting to look like I'd be working harder than I ever had in my life. Only you know what? Once the decisions were made, I found myself looking forward to it.

Partly I looked forward to doing the work because for the first time I could see far enough ahead to know it needn't go on forever. The work now would give me loafing time later on, or so I figured.

Point being, looking forward to anything makes time go by with about as much speed as a turtle walking on ice. But slow or fast, time passes, and so it did here. Riding out and finding Darby Sullivan, I made plans to ride down to Tucson with him and take a look at the mules and wagons once we had the mortgage business out of the way.

Getting that done proved not to be much trouble. Mr. Wilcox had some papers drawn up; me, Billy, and Johnny all signed them. He up and handed us three thousand dollars once that was done. Then we signed some more papers, gave him back two thousand dollars, and we had that land out yonder tied up for four months.

Mr. Wilcox told us we ought to read through the contracts careful before signing them, and even said we ought to get a lawyer to do it for us. We didn't. We could all write our names, and we could all read a little . . . Johnny the best, I reckon, but hadn't none of us seen words like those on the papers we signed.

We talked it over, and figured since Mr. Wilcox had told us we ought to get a lawyer, he probably wasn't hiding nothing, so we went ahead and signed on the spot.

With the paper signing out of the way, we went down to the smithy and sat down to talk things over. Pooling our money, including the thousand dollars we pocketed at the bank, I was surprised to find out how much we still had. With every cent all in a pile, it came to twenty-four hundred dollars and change.

After some thought, we each pocketed two hundred for expense money, and I slipped the remaining eighteen hundred in my pocket, thinking to work out a deal for the mules and wagons with it.

Now, at any other time in our lives, that much money would have made us feel richer than Jay Gould himself. But when we stacked it up against what we'd have to pay to get started in the freighting business, and against the ten

thousand we still needed to buy that land, it seemed a piti-
ful amount.

We still had the smithy, though, and if we kept it going
whenever possible, that would give us a bit of steady
money. And Johnny was going out after those horses. Even
if he brought back only half of what he wanted, it would
add considerably to our wad of cash.

At best, it was shaping up to be a big job. Maybe one
bigger then we could sink our teeth into. But if hard work
could make it happen, we stood a chance.

Johnny was anxious to take off into the wild country so
he could get started on building the fence sections to trap
those mustangs, but Billy had figured to ride with me
down to Tucson.

"Guess I'd best stay here," Billy said. The work kept piling up at the smithy, and try as we might, we couldn't get
ahead of it. "We close this place up for more'n two days,
we would have to get somebody to take care of the horses,
and the backed-up work would drown us."

So in the end, that was the way of it. Johnny went out for
the mustangs, Billy kept working at the smithy, and I went
riding down to Tucson with Darby Sullivan to see the
Widow Richardson. With only two of us on the trail, we
rode cautious, keeping our mouths closed and our eyes
open. We didn't see much of anything the whole way, except a few rabbits and a bunch of snakes.

Before we reached the outskirts of Tucson, Darby had
me expecting to see Paradise. Tucson turned out to be just
another town, though a hectically busy one. We stopped
off in town to clear away some of the trail dust before
going out to see the Widow Richardson, and it seemed natural to cut the inside dust first.

We found a saloon and ordered whiskey with a beer
chaser. It wasn't much past noon, and close to ninety in the
shade, but though the streets were busy, the saloon was

near empty. A couple of fancy-dressed whores sat at a table but didn't so much as stir when we came in.

Way we were dressed, and the amount of trail dust on us, it might be they figured we didn't have enough money to be worth saddling up to. Truth is, I didn't much mind. I was tired, thirsty, hungry, and in no mood for anything except taking care of business.

We had our drinks, then found a barbershop and took a long bath. Darby ended it there, but I changed into fresh clothes, then went ahead and had myself a shave and a haircut. I let the barber take off my mustache while he was at it. He ended by splashing me with some kind of smell-good, and I went out of there feeling cocky as a banty rooster.

We got us a bite to eat, then rode out to see the widow. Turned out there wasn't much to see. She had herself a small house that needed a coat of paint, a barn that someone had started but never quite finished, and a corral big enough to hold a herd of mules. The corral was empty.

The wagons, two big Pittsburghs, along with a pair of trailer wagons, sat beside the half-completed barn. The sun and the rain hadn't done them much good. I didn't know what kind of husband, nor what kind of muleskinner, Jobe Richardson had been, but he apparently wasn't much on keeping things in good repair.

The Widow Richardson—she told us her name was Callie—showed signs of having been a lovely woman. Darby told me she wasn't but forty, though I'd have guessed fifteen years beyond that. The wind, sun, and rigors of a hard life had left their mark on her, aging her skin and turning her hair gray before her time.

Even her eyes seemed flat and lifeless, showing a spark only when Darby mentioned her husband.

"Jobe was a good man," she said. "Nothing ever seemed to work out for him, and he was prone to grabbing on to bigger steers than he could throw, but he never gave up on trying."

She invited us inside for coffee, and we accepted. Once inside the house, we met her children, and despite Callie Richardson's age, the oldest child wasn't yet nine. She ran them all outside, poured us coffee, and we sat down at the table.

We talked for a time, then finally came to the wagons and mules. "Jobe fenced in a section of land right out behind the barn a piece," she said. "I had the boys run all the mules out there so they could fend for themselves.

"The truth is, they're running to skin and bones, but there's nothing wrong with them that a week or so of good feed wouldn't cure."

I finished off the coffee, stood up. "I 'spect we best look things over before we go talking price."

We went out and did just that. I didn't like anything I saw. All the wagons were old, and one had a bed that was suffering to the point of being ready to give way. It would have to be replaced before I'd trust the wagon to hold a load of freight.

Jobe Richardson might have been as good a man as Callie said, but I'd swear he hadn't once oiled the hubs on those wagons. Between the wagons and the trailers, there were sixteen wheels, and it looked to me like every one would have to be greased, and at least two needed to be replaced.

The barn was packed full of harness, stay chains, and other gear, and while most of it was in better shape than the wagons, there was work to be done there, as well. Then we went out to see the mules.

Right off, I knew that's where the money would be well spent. The mules were skinny from lack of good feed, but they were big, strong, Missouri mules to the last.

Once the looking was done, we went back into the house

and had another cup of coffee. "Mrs. Richardson," I said, "Darby tells me you're askin' twenty-five hundred for the wagons and mules?"

She picked up a dishrag and wiped at the table. "He said they were worth as much."

"They might be," I said. "The wagons all need work, and some of the gear needs mending, but the mules are all fine. Might be Darby's right.

"Thing is, I plain ain't got that much cash, ma'am. If you think it fair, I can give half the price up front, and pay the rest off as we go. I could give you sixty a month, and pay off the balance at the end of a year."

Again she wiped at a table that was already spotless.

"I was married to Jobe for almost thirteen years," she said at last. "For most of that time we never saw more than thirty dollars at one time. About three years ago, Jobe came into a small inheritance. He put it in the bank, then worked like a dog for two years adding to it.

"He started buying mules when he could find a good one, and finally he put together a freight outfit. He was so sure that this time he'd make money. I think he would have, except for getting himself killed.

"I know those wagons are in poor shape, Mr. Hawkins, but don't think poorly of Jobe because of that. He bought good mules, but by then the money was gone, and those wagons were all he could afford. Given a little time, he would have fixed them up proper.

"I'll accept your offer, Mr. Hawkins. You may not know it, but even the twelve hundred and fifty dollars is more than twice what Murphy offered, and more than enough to take care of my children."

Mrs. Richardson stood up and walked to the window. She looked out for half a minute, then turned back to me. "I want to live in a town, Mr. Hawkins. I want neighbors to talk to and stores to shop in. Your money will let me do that. Give me the twelve hundred and fifty dollars, Mr.

Hawkins, and I'll let you know where you may send the rest."

That was the way of it. Using a receipt book of her husband's, Mrs. Richardson wrote me out a bill of sale, I gave her the money, and that was that.

Well, not quite, maybe. There was still the task of getting wagons and mules back to Globe, and that was no easy thing. Darby looked over the wagons with a fresh eye, now that the sale was made.

"They'll make it back to Globe, I reckon," he said. "Long as we're running empty. We get 'em back there, though, and they'll sure stand some work."

"Seems like you're singing a different tune, now that you got your cut of the sale."

Darby spat, mumbled something I couldn't understand. I asked what it was, and he looked up at me with a frown of pure pain written across his face. "I said I didn't take no money from the widder."

"I thought you had a deal with her."

"I did. Only when it come down to it, I couldn't take the money. Just seemed like she needed it more'n I did, is all."

"By God," I said. "I never figured a crochety old fart like you would have a soft spot for a widow woman."

"I never figured it neither," Darby said. "And don't you go working your jaws about it. It's going to take a weeklong drunk to make me forget about it now."

Darby spent the rest of the afternoon teaching me how to get the mules in the traces and showing me how to handle the big wagon. I'd thought it'd be tough learning, and parts of it were. Only once he got started, I found it was a good bit like handling the mules that pulled the artillery back in the army.

We worked all evening, then settled into the barn for the night. Come morning, Mrs. Richardson fed us a good breakfast, and we began stringing mules out in front of those wagons. Darby hitched up eight mules per wagon, even though the wagon was empty, figuring to teach me how to run a full string of mules.

And at that, it took better than two hours to get everything together. By then my shirt was soaked through with sweat, and I was madder than a wet hen. I let out a string of cuss words and tried planting my boot in a mule's rear end.

The mule sidestepped, and my other foot came out from under me. I hit the ground hard enough to raise a cloud of dust, and Darby went to guffawing.

"What the hell are you laughing at?" I asked.

"If you was lookin' at things from here," he said, "you'd know damned well what I'm laughing at. Truth is, you ain't coming along too bad. You got the cussin' pure perfect. Some mightn't agree, but any skinner will tell you a mule understands getting swore at quicker'n anything. That's half the fight, right there.

"I got a strong feeling it's gonna be a spell before you're up to hauling a load of freight, though."

I sat up in the dust, took off my hat, wiped sweat away from my forehead with the sleeve of my shirt. "How long you figure?"

"You mean to get you haulin' freight proper?"

"Yes, sir. Me and the others."

Darby scratched at the stubble on his jaw. "I don't expect you'll be true if you call yourself a skinner before the summer's out," he said. "But if you got a good swamper who can show you the ropes, and keep you from making yourself any more the fool than you already are—hell, I don't know. Two weeks. Maybe three."

"I guess that ain't so bad. It'll take a week to get these wagons in shape, and a week more to fatten up the mules."

"That ain't the important part," Darby said. "A business like this ain't no good less'n folks know about it. You got to have somebody out beating the bushes, looking for loads until enough folks know you well enough to come askin' on their own.

"First, though, you got to figure how much you'll

charge, and that ain't always easy. Too much, and you won't get no loads. Too little, and you'll go broke."

"Murphy gets away with charging plenty."

"That's cause he's got the only freighting outfit in these parts. You want to take his business, you'll have to charge a sight less."

"That shouldn't be hard."

Darby grinned. "No, sir, I'd say not. You could cut Murphy's prices by half, and still make a good profit."

"Might be we'll do that," I said. "Might be we'll do just that."

"He'll be real unhappy, if you do."

"That bother you?"

Darby's grin turned into a chuckle. "Bother me, hell. It tickles me."

Once we had the mules ready, we climbed up onto the driver's seat and Darby showed me how to handle the trace lines. "Sooner or later, you'll need to handle a whip," he said, "but right now you'd likely take out your own eye. Give me that canvas bag there."

The canvas bag Darby wanted was hung from a nail right near where I sat. Darby took it and climbed down. Scouting around, he filled it near full up with rocks about half the size of a good biscuit. He handed the heavy bag up to me.

"Hang it there in easy reach," he said. "Them lead mules won't get up and go, whomp 'em in the rear with a rock.

"Don't fling 'em none too gentle, neither. You want them mules to do what you say, you got to get their attention. Sometimes a string of good swear words'll get the job done. Most times you need a whip or a rock."

"I'm already starting to wish I'd never laid eyes on a mule," I said.

"You won't like 'em no better as time goes on. Now, if you think you can handle that wagon, we'd best get on our way."

"I'm as ready as I'm gonna get."

Darby cracked his whip, I flung a couple of rocks, and we rolled out. Globe seemed a damned sight farther away than it had earlier, and long before the trip was over, I was dead certain I'd chose the wrong business.

I don't know what gave us the most trouble, the mules that were pulling, or the thirty-four strung out behind. We also had our horses tied along with the mules, but that didn't work out a bit. They didn't like the mules, the mules didn't like them, and I was beginning to hate them all.

Three times that first day, my mules got tangled in their traces, and Darby had to wade in and straighten things out. On top of it all, every damned wheel on every damned wagon squeaked loud enough to wake the dead. By the time we made camp, it occurred to me that the smartest thing to do would be to jump on Nugget's back, point his nose west, and not look back until we ran into ocean.

What I did instead was spend near two hours watering and staking out the mules. Then I crawled into the back of a wagon and went to sleep without even eating supper or drinking a cup of coffee. Darby woke me up at first light. We ate, then started the whole thing over again.

CHAPTER 10

ONCE WE FINALLY reached Globe, I was ready to burn the wagons and shoot dead every blasted mule I'd bought. We'd taken our sweet time on the return trip, and Darby had taught me all he could about handling a mule team. It helped me, I reckon, but it didn't do a thing to improve the disposition of those mules.

Even so, after all the time spent on the trail with me, Darby claimed those mules were gentle and sweet as a eight-year-old girl compared to me. Might be he wasn't too far wrong.

It was well into evening when we pulled up, but Billy still had the smithy open, though he was sitting out front taking a breather when we rolled into town. Johnny was already gone out into the wild nowhere, and by then was likely in the process of building his fence sections.

Billy stood up as we drove closer, looked up at me. "By God, Ben," he said, "you look like hell. A body would think the mules were driving an' you was pulling."

"That's how it feels."

Climbing down, I stretched out my back. Every damn time one of those wagon wheels hit a little rut, it felt like a ten-foot drop, and I'd have swore my spine had been ground to dust. I walked around the wagons with Billy.

Finally, Billy spat into the dust. "They ain't much, are they?"

"They'll stand some work, I guess."

"Mules look good, but we'll play hell keeping them all in that little corral."

It was plain we hadn't thought things all the way

through. While trying to talk me into buying the mules and wagons, Darby had allowed that there was plenty of room at the smithy to corral the mules and stow the wagons. There wasn't.

We could get the fifty mules into the corral, all right, but we'd have to squeeze them together like beans in a pot. Nor did we have a place to stow enough hay to feed them. And those wagons needed a spot out of the rain and sun until we got them fixed up, or when they weren't in use. Which all meant we had plenty of work yet to do.

"The corral will do for a few days. I figure we can stretch it out to the south. You got any idea who owns that land back behind the smithy?"

"No, sir. But it looks like we'll need some of it. By God, Ben, are you sure this was the right move?"

I shrugged. "It's the horse we saddled. Guess we'll have to see if we can ride it."

While we were standing around talking, P. G. Murphy happened to walk by. Might be I wouldn't have noticed him, except he was laughing like he'd lost his senses. He was all the way across the street, but his booming laugh carried the distance with ease.

"What the hell are you laughing at!" I yelled.

He was laughing so hard he had trouble answering me. "That . . . that's your . . . freighting outfit!" He started laughing again, waved a hand at me in dismissal, then strode off, still guffawing like a crazy jackass.

"Wonder if he could laugh with a big fist planted in his mouth," I said.

Darby pulled a plug of tobacco from his pocket, worried at it with his teeth until he had a piece pulled loose. He chewed a second, moved the chaw over into his jaw, spat. "Let's just take his business away," he said. "We'll see how loud he laughs at that."

I nodded. "Guess that's the best way to go about it. All right, let's crowd them mules into the corral, then get ourselves some decent food. Come morning we'll start working on getting these wagons in shape."

After we put the mules in the corral, we tossed in most of the hay we had, then went on down to Molly's. We ate our fill, topped it off with a few beers at O'Brien's, then settled in to sleep. Come morning we started working harder than any mule.

First we went looking for whoever owned the land back behind the smithy. We found him without trouble, but he could see for himself how much we needed the land, and wasn't much on dickering. His name was Wilbur Kidwell, and he owned the feed and grain store down at the other end of town.

"I own exactly two acres of land there," he said. "I want fifty an acre. All or none."

We tried talking him down, but he wasn't having any. We had no choice but to pay his price. I peeled off the money. Once the land was ours, I called him a greedy son of a bitch. It didn't ruffle a feather. "Might be I am," he said. "But you're the fool who paid my price."

Well, he had me there.

We set to work then, and if time had been passing slow, of a sudden it was flying past. We worked from sunup to dark seven days a week, and next thing I knew I looked up and three weeks had passed.

Right at the start, we sat down and worked up a price list, cutting Murphy's prices by a third. It still seemed like a lot to charge folks, but Darby allowed they wouldn't look at it that way.

Me, Billy, and a couple of roustabouts we'd hired had done near all the work. Darby had spent most of his time drumming up business by word of mouth and by placing an ad in the newspaper and by tacking up fliers everywhere he could find a place. And I had to admit that having worked for Murphy, Darby knew where the customers were, and he was right about the prices.

Some folks were reluctant to trust loads to an unknown company, but it was that or pay Murphy's prices. Before you could say scat, Darby had a month's business lined up.

And we'd sure as hell done plenty of work in those three weeks. We more than tripled the size of the corral, added a long roof line to the smithy so we could shelter the wagons from rain, set us up a place to store hay, and fixed up those wagons so they were almighty pretty.

We also gave that little sleeping room an outside door, slipped a desk and chair inside, and called it an office. It wasn't much, but it was all we figured to need.

In honor of Dunie, we painted both wagons green, had a painter put our names on the side, and just like that, we were ready for business.

Every day he was in town, Darby spent a few hours teaching me and Billy all the ins and outs of hauling freight, including how to use an eighteen-foot bullwhip. Darby could flick a fly off a mule's ear without hurting the mule, but for a time there, me and Billy were plain dangerous.

It took a good long time before we could even crack those whips, except by accident. Once the day's work was done, though, we'd spend an hour or so practicing, and while we still weren't safe to be around, we did get to the point where we could at least crack the whip close to a mule without hurting it—or any fool dumb enough to stand close.

All this time, we'd been doing our best to keep up with the smithy business. We didn't quite do it, but we came close enough to keep most of our customers happy.

Along toward the end of that third week, Murphy started walking by a couple of times a day. And he'd stopped laughing. I reckon part of it was all the work we'd put in. We looked like a freighting outfit now, even if we hadn't yet hauled a single load.

But I suspect the biggest part of it was all the customers

Darby had been lining up. By that time, I allowed that at least a couple must have told Murphy where he could stick his price list, and if they had, Murphy might soon go on the warpath.

We finished that three weeks of backbreaking work on a Friday, and figuring to rest up a couple of days before getting back to work again. Once dark had settled in proper, we went down to O'Brien's and flopped into chairs. I was wore to a frazzle.

A shot of whiskey and a beer helped, but I figured it'd take about twelve hours' sleep to get me going again.

Alice came over and sat down, telling us that Joanie had quit. Some cowboy had swept her off her feet and they were to get married the following week. Dunie had hired a new girl that very day, and Alice called her over.

She was a pretty redhead named Samantha Hall, and folks all called her Sam. Sam wasn't no bigger than a minute, but she had the size where it counted.

I bought her and Alice both a drink, and Alice winked at me. "You've gone through the rest of us like a longhorn bull in heifer heaven. You'd best give Sam a whirl quick, else you'll ruin your record."

I grinned, looked at Sam, then at Alice. "I'd sure like to, but I'm so tired I can't raise my eyebrows, much less anything else."

"Bet you ten dollars you're wrong," Sam said.

Well, sir, I looked Sam over again. While I was looking, she licked her lips and gave me a smile that was purely wicked.

"Guess I'll take that bet."

She took hold of my hand and led me upstairs. That was the first time in my life I lost a bet with a smile on my face.

Come morning, we had our first walk-in customer. Two, in fact. The first fellow that came asking was a big, hard-striding rancher named Allen Patterson.

"I've started a ranch about forty miles west of Flagstaff,"

he said, "and I'm planning on putting up a house that'll be the envy of the whole damn territory. My wife wants it, and by God, she's going to get it.

"I have three thousand pounds of foofaraw sitting in Santa Fe, everything from fancy mirrors to mahogany, and that son-of-a-bitch Murphy wants more to haul it the rest of the way than it cost to begin with. And at that, he won't take it no farther than Flagstaff."

We sat down and went to dickering, which mostly consisted of Darby fiddling with a pencil and paper. I don't know if he knew what he was doing or not, but Patterson must have thought so. Anyway, when Darby finally looked up from his scratching and quoted a price, it near made me choke, but Patterson took it in stride.

"That still ain't cheap," he said, "but it's a damn sight less than what Murphy asked. How do you want to be paid?"

"Half now, half on delivery," I said. "Anything we break or damage we'll pay for. Anything that might have been broke when we pick up the load is your loss."

"That's fair, I guess."

Patterson took a thick roll of bills from his pocket and peeled off half the freighting charges. He went on out, and I looked at the money. "Might be we got a chance, after all," I said. "Folks keep paying like this, and we'll sure turn a nice profit.

"You can't count no profit until the freight's delivered," Darby said. "There's a lot that can happen between picking up a load and getting it where it goes."

"I reckon there is," I said. "A man makes a tall target sitting up on one of those wagons."

"Been wanting to talk to you about that," Darby said. "Let's go outside, and I'll show you a little trick."

Darby led the way out to the wagons, and we climbed up into the bed of the nearest. "What you do," he said, "is put a plank partition right here just a bit over two feet behind the driver's seat. Bolt an iron plate over each side that's thick enough to stop a bullet, and you'll have a cubbyhole that two men can drop back into.

"Stow some water, a bit of food, and some spare ammunition in here, and you're all set. Somebody starts shooting at you, drop in here and you can hold off an army."

"Does Murphy run his wagons that way?"

"Hell no, he don't. It cuts into hauling space. One of these wagons will haul twenty-five hundred pounds—three thousand, if it's in good enough shape and you pack in proper. Depending on what you're hauling, this little space cuts that by three, four hundred pounds, meaning it cuts down on profit a touch.

"Most loads are based on weight, and you got space left over, even after spreading out three thousand pounds. But some loads you do lose freight, and that's enough to turn Murphy agin it. Point being, Murphy won't let his men fix up their wagons this way."

"Hell, it won't take but a couple of hours to set up both wagons," I said. "We'll do it."

"You gave in on that quick," Darby said. "I argued myself blue with Murphy, and he never gave an inch."

"Might be because he hires his driving done," I said. "I'm going to be sitting up on that seat myself. Somebody goes to shooting, I'd dig my own hole in the freight."

We got to work on the cubbyholes right off. While we were at it, our second customer came calling. This one had the strangest request I could figure. Even Darby claimed he'd never hauled such.

This was a fellow named Clive Toschlog, and he, too, was a rancher. "I don't have a lot of land," he said, "and truth be known, I'm short on money. Figuring to make the most of what I got, I bought myself a hundred head of the best breeding stock to be found.

"Thing is, my bull up and died on me. I bought another from a fellow up in Colorado. What I was wondering is, can you all haul a bull in one of those big wagons?"

Me an' Darby looked at each other, then back at him. "Are you funning us?" I asked.

"Not a whit."

"I don't see why we can't haul a bull," Darby said. "But why not just trail him along? We'd have to charge you three times what a bull's worth."

"Not three times what this one's worth," Toschlog said. "He cost me a thousand dollars all by himself."

"A thousand dollars! You paid a thousand dollars for one bull?"

"Yes, sir, I did. And cheap at the price. This bull's already won prizes all over. What with the heifers I already have, I figure to have that bull sire the best damned herd of cattle this side of the Mississippi.

"Three, maybe four years from now, I figure to be a rich man. But first I got to get that bull close enough to my heifers to get the job done. And you can see why I don't want to trail him along like a ten-dollar cow."

"A thousand . . . yes, sir, I guess I do."

We worked out a deal, and our second load was lined up.

We still had plenty of things to figure, such as who'd go after what load, and what we'd do with the smithy while me and Billy were both gone, but things were starting to move. And I was already seeing a problem I hadn't counted on at all. What with the loads Darby had lined up during his riding, we were already facing more business than we could easily handle.

Most folks were patient. Darby lined the loads up so we could make a couple of long runs, then several shorter ones, and he told folks it might be several weeks before we could get to them.

But if we wanted enough business to buy that land out yonder, and enough to cut deep into Murphy's stranglehold, I could see the time ahead when we'd need to add a couple of wagons to our string. Two or three more wagons, another fifty or sixty mules, a couple of drivers and swampers, and well, you see my point.

Here we hadn't hauled a damned pound of freight, and we'd already outgrown ourselves. Hell of a thing.

All in all, things were going along pretty smooth. Maybe too smooth. I'd never had a streak of good luck that lasted so long in my life. I should've known it was going to break.

CHAPTER 11

STILL, OUR LUCK did hold for a spell . . . First thing we had to do was hire ourselves another man or two. We needed another swamper, and it was in my mind to hire somebody permanent to watch over the smithy during those times when me and Billy were both gone.

We found a swamper easy enough, a young Missourian named Douglas Poe. He'd been in or around Globe nearly two months, but hadn't found much in the way of steady work. He had worked at one of the copper mines for a while but didn't like anything about it.

He claimed not to mind the work, but didn't like being tied down to one spot. He'd thought to hire on with one of the local ranchers, or maybe even the stageline. Billy got to talking to him one day and finally brought him over to the smithy. We talked a time, me and Billy powwowed, and we ended up offering him a job.

We offered twice what he could make as a cowpuncher or a stage driver, and he snapped it up.

Finding somebody to keep an eye on the smithy and watch the freight office was trickier. The main thing we needed was somebody who could not only spend time at the place, but somebody with enough school learning to write down orders and keep the books in order.

That, and somebody honest enough to be trusted with money. They would need to take payment on freight orders, put money in a bank account we'd started, and generally be trustworthy.

Finding such a person in a town like Globe wasn't all that difficult, but finding one not already employed somewhere was another thing altogether. We finally settled on a spinster woman named Helen Decker. She had worked down at the mercantile, but had been forced to quit a couple of years earlier to care for her sister. The sister had since died, but the mercantile hadn't held her job.

I explained to her that while the work itself wouldn't be difficult, some of the men she would be around might be. She allowed rough language and drunken men wouldn't bother her, and lacking any other folks lining up for the job, we decided to hire her.

Helen was fifty-three years old and wore a kind of pinched look on her face, but Darby seemed taken with her right off.

That being accomplished, we set off to handle our first loads. Me and Darby went off on the Santa Fe run, while Billy and Douglas Poe headed north to pick up the thousand-dollar bull.

By the time me and Darby had been on the trail a few days, it seemed the ways of the mules, and the manner of handling a big wagon, suddenly started to make sense to me. Might be part of it was getting the hang of using a whip and of flinging a rock so it would smack solid into the arse of whatever mule I chose.

Not that I didn't lose my temper a time or two, and not that I didn't make the air boil with cussing out those mules. Only I enjoyed being out there under the open sky and, even though riding that big wagon was enough to shatter a man's spine, it was still a whole damn sight better than punching another man's cows.

And we were traveling in better style than any cowpuncher. A cowboy carries what he can stuff into his saddlebags or wrap in his bedroll. Food comes from a chuck wagon, and I'd never known a cook who was generous in doling out anything more than beans and biscuits.

We'd brought along plenty of food: flour, meal, bacon, coffee, sugar, salt pork, beans, and a big helping of canned peaches and tomatoes. We'd also brought a skillet, a big iron kettle, tin cups, tin plates, forks and spoons, a coffeepot, and a bucket for hauling water.

We'd also brought along extra hickory spokes for the wheels, spare links of chain, and even a spanking-new wagon tongue. Darby had bought asnaburg sheets that were double layered, and had mackinaw blankets sewed between the two layers. These we'd use to cover the wagons once the cargo was loaded.

And I'll tell you what . . . those big Pittsburgh wagons were almighty pretty the way we'd painted them up. They were built with a high prow and high stern and curved sides just like a sailing ship. They were also watertight, and when need be, you could float them across a fair-sized river.

We picked up the freight in Santa Fe without any trouble, spent the night in town, then started back out on the trail. We were near halfway back when our spell of good luck finally broke.

We'd followed the Butterfield route up to Santa Fe, but we figured to cut a full week off the return journey by heading pretty much due west on the return trip. Darby had claimed those wagons would ride smoother when loaded, and he was right. That being the case, I pushed along as hard as we dared, and we made decent time.

Then, not far from Indian Wells, it happened. We were riding along peaceful as you please, and just like that an Indian reared up from nowhere and cut loose with a rifle.

Thing that saved us was the time. It was a bit past noon and I'd been looking for a spot to swing off the trail so we could build a fire for coffee and a bite to eat. I saw a likely spot, and swung the mule team that way. Near as I could figure, that Indian must have thought we'd seen him and were trying to reach cover, so he up and fired too soon.

His first bullet smacked into the seat right between me and Darby, tearing deep into the wood and sending a couple of splinters flying, one of which sliced into my cheek. Not even knowing if they could pull a load like we had at a run, I snapped that long bullwhip and yelled like a madman. Those mules broke into a run, pointing right at a shallow wash.

We went into the wash and I got the mules stopped. Even before I had, Darby had already jumped back into that space we'd made behind the seat. About that time three or four other Indians cut loose, and I jumped in beside Darby with bullets flying all around me.

We'd added a platform to the bottom of that space so as to be high enough to shoot proper, but we ducked down our heads and kept them down till the firing let up a bit. Only then did we peek up to see where those Indians might be situated.

At first I saw nothing, and then the sun glinted off something in the rocks seventy, maybe eighty yards off. I squeezed off three rounds at the spot, and an Indian jumped up and dove into better cover. A bullet whumped into the wagon right below my chest, but the thick wood and iron plate we'd bolted to it stopped any real damage.

About the only thing we had going for us was the fact that we were reasonably well protected, and we had a decent field of fire. Instead of putting those heavy sheets up on stays like you'd see on a settlers wagon, we'd stretched them across the freight and lashed them down.

Hadn't been for that, we'd have been near blind to anything happening behind us. As it was, we could see over the freight without exposing ourselves too much, so we settled in to wait.

There was one high outcropping of rock about two hundred yards off to the west, and that worried me a bit. Should one of those Indians get up there, he might be able to shoot right down into our cubbyhole. I pointed it out to Darby.

"Seen it," he said. "There's no telling how far this wash runs, neither. They work around and get down in it, they might get up close afore we see 'em."

I hadn't thought about that. Rearing up enough to see, I took a look down the wash. It took a sharp turn no more than thirty yards away, and like Darby said, there was no telling how far it ran.

"I'm beginning to think running in here was a mistake," I said. "How many you figure are out there?"

Darby dug into a bag and pulled out two strips of jerky. He handed one to me, worked at the other a minute before speaking. "Can't say for sure. No more than four or five. But it's a good bet they get help afore we do. And I 'spect pulling in here was the wisest move. Fact is, I allowed you run in here to protect the mules."

"Never gave the mules a thought. Just seemed like the best cover around."

"Well, better to be lucky than smart. If you hadn't run in here, those Indians would've started shooting the mules right off, and then we'd be in a worse pickle than this."

"Damn it to hell!" I said. Biting off a big piece of jerky, I worked at it with my teeth. It was like chewing the sole of an old boot, but at least it gave me something to do.

After a time I noticed Darby was having a hard time standing still, and his face was screwed up into a mask of discomfort. "What's ailing you?" I asked. "You gettin' restless?"

"Hell no, I ain't gettin' restless. Least no more'n you'd expect."

"Then what's put ants in your pants?"

"There's about to be something besides ants in there. I got to take care of my animal economy, else you ain't gonna want to stay in this wagon with me much longer."

"You got to what?"

"You heard me."

"You can't hold it back?"

"Been holding it back two hours now. Another five minutes, and I'll be filling my drawers right here."

"I swear to God, I never knowed a man who needed to empty his bowels so often. It ain't no wonder you're skinny."

"Better'n being bound up. Most times, anyway. Besides, all them damn Mexican strawberries I ate last night ain't helping the cause none."

"I ate as many beans as you did, and you don't see me about to fill my drawers."

"Reckon you got more room to hold it. Anyway, I got to try and sneak down off this wagon, else those Indians are going to be the least of our worries."

"Hell's bells! All right, you go on ahead. I reckon it's safe enough, long as you stay low. Climbing out of this cubbyhole, and gettin' back in will be the hard part."

"Guess I can manage it."

"Watch yourself."

Darby gave me a look. "I ain't about to get shot while squatting down and doing my business. You jest keep that rifle to hand."

I nodded, and Darby made ready to jump out. With one quick leap, he jumped up and swung over the side. It must have taken the Indians by surprise, 'cause they didn't let go a shot. I stuck my head up over the side enough to look down at Darby.

"Downwind," I said. "Go downwind."

"I'm going to that clump of brush down the draw there," he said. "I don't give a damn which way the wind's a-blowing."

Running low, Darby trotted to a clump of brush about twenty yards down the draw. I kept my own rifle at the ready, but once he squatted down the mules blocked him from my view. Five minutes passed, and then he raised up enough so I could see him again.

He buttoned up his pants, slipped his suspenders up over his shoulders, and started trotting back to the wagon. He hadn't taken more than four loping steps when two Indians came charging around the bend in the wash.

Snapping my rifle up, I squeezed off a round, and the first Indian spun around and dropped. The second Indian fired and I heard Darby yelp. I fired again . . . too quick. My bullet kicked dust up between the Indian's feet.

He fired a second time, and one of the lead mules reared up and squealed, then collapsed in a heap. Before I could fire a third time, the Indian ducked back around the bend. Keeping my rifle on the spot, I yelled out for Darby. Just as I yelled, his head popped up over the side of the wagon, and he flung himself over the side and into the cubbyhole.

"Thought they nailed you sure," I said.

Darby wiped at a bloody streak along the side of his neck. "Close," he said. "They come too damned close."

A rifle boomed and another mule screamed and went to bucking. A second shot knocked the mule down. Darby fired three quick shots. "One of 'em made it up onto those high rocks," he said. "Now we got trouble."

I thought a minute. If we stayed put, those Indians would likely pick us to pieces. I couldn't see but one way out.

"There's one dead yonder," I said. "There's a second around the bend, and a third up in those rocks. I don't think there's more'n one other out there."

"That's a-plenty."

"I'm going out there among them," I said.

Darby took his eyes off those high-up rocks just long enough to scowl at me. "I don't think that's such a good idea," he said. "I got a notion those are Zuni out there. Ain't nothing this side of hell worse'n an Apache, 'cepting one thing, and that's a Zuni."

"Don't know nothing about them."

"They're good people," Darby said. "I been among 'em.

But when it comes to fighting, you take an Apache, mix in a handful of scorpions, three or four rattlesnakes, and you got a Zuni. Might be we ain't got much chance sitting here, but you go out there, and folks won't find nothing but your bones."

"You got any better idea?"

Darby spat a brown stream of tobacco juice, then rubbed his hand across his mouth. "Yes, sir, I have. I say we ought to make a run for it. Stretch them reins up here, hunker down, and hope we get away afore those Zuni can shoot too many mules."

"Two things wrong with that," I said. "In the first place, we ain't going nowhere without cutting those dead mules free. Second thing is, I'm not so sure we can get this big bastard of a wagon backed out of here without hooking the mules up behind and pulling it back."

"By God," Darby said. "I hadn't thought of that. We are kind of jammed in this wash, ain't we?"

"You know it. I got to do it, Darby. I got to go out there and try to even the odds."

"Well, it's been nice knowing you, Hawkins."

"You just keep that one high up in the rocks there pinned down."

I let my eyes run over the area, picking out likely cover here and there. It was all a mixture of rocks, brush, washes, and large areas of flat nothing. "See where that rock kind of juts out toward us over yonder there?"

Darby raised his head. "Sure. What about it?"

"See how it trails straight up to that high ledge? If I could get up there I'd have that fellow in the wash cold. Might be I could get in a good shot at the one high up there, too."

"You might, but how you gonna get there?"

"That one in the wash won't be able to see me, and you can keep the other fellow pinned down."

"That's assuming that Zuni in the wash stayed put after

the shooting. And I figure there's one other out there somewheres. Like as not, he's just lying in wait, hoping one of us will do something foolish."

It was hot, and getting hotter with each passing minute. A hundred degrees, I figured, and maybe a bit better. We had two big canteens of water in there with us, and part of a third under the seat. Enough to last us a full two days. And we had food in plenty.

Neither of which meant a damn thing. Come dark, those Indians could sneak right down close and likely kill us before we knew they were near. And even if we did survive the night, come daylight they'd begin sharping away at the mules again.

No, sir. The way it was, we were letting those Zuni make all the moves. Staying alive meant forcing them to change the way they were thinking. And the only way to do that was for me to get out there among them.

Filling my pockets with cartridges, I grabbed up one of the canteens and a bag full of jerky. "Draw a bead on the last spot you saw that Indian up yonder," I said. "You see anything at all, go to shooting, and don't stop till that rifle runs empty."

"You can count on me. Luck, Hawkins."

I nodded. A trickle of sweat ran down into my eye, stinging enough to make me try to blink it away. I didn't want to go over the side of that wagon. Just at the thought of it, my stomach was churning like I'd drunk sour milk. Only a damned fool would go out into the rocks looking to fight any kind of Indian.

This was their country, and they moved through it like ghosts. I'd done my share of fighting, and I'd stalked wild game any number of times. But here I was out of my class, and I knew it.

My only hope was to take them by surprise. The last thing in the world they'd be expecting was me running out there like a madman, hoping to get up in those rocks. Or so I figured. If I was right, might be I could catch one or two of them by surprise and get us out of the fix we were in.

I glanced both ways down the trail, hoping to see a troop of horse cavalry riding toward us, I guess. But I saw only the sun, the sand, and the rocks.

"You got that rifle pointed?" I asked.

"It's ready."

"So am I, I reckon. Here we go."

Taking a deep breath, I grabbed the top board of the wagon and swung myself up and over. My foot came down on the edge of the big wheel, and from there I jumped on down to the ground and went to running.

Behind me I heard Darby's rifle booming out shot after shot. I headed straight for the outcropping of sand-colored rock, running for all I was worth.

I hadn't made more than a dozen strides when a rifle shot rang out from over to the east. The bullet kicked dust three feet in front of me. Two more strides and then something wicked struck me high on the hip. Only an instant after the bullet struck, I heard the sharp retort of the rifle.

The impact knocked me sideways, and I stumbled and fell. I struck the ground hard, losing my grip on the rifle, and every bit of air in my lungs.

CHAPTER 12

MY WHOLE HIP was throbbing to beat the band, and I could hardly breathe. But there wasn't any time at all to determine how badly I was hurt. Grabbing up my rifle, I ran for the rocks. My hip and side hurt like a son of a bitch, and didn't want to move proper. I was gasping for air that wouldn't come. And I was scared.

A bullet whipped by me, so close I felt the air of it. A second bullet slapped the rifle from my hands, and though it was the wrong thing to do, I stopped half a second to scoop it up.

Then the rock outcropping was right there in front of me. I dove in behind a horse-sized boulder and just stayed right there for a couple of minutes, fighting at the pain and trying to get my mind working.

I'd been hit by a bullet. How bad was I wounded? Where were the Indians? How many of them had seen me make that run? Were they even now working around to get a shot at me?

Questions flooded my mind, but I had no answers. There was only the pain, and the almost animallike fear. *Move.* I had to move deeper into the rocks. Deeper and higher. It was the only chance I had.

I forced myself to my feet and started working through the rocks, climbing as I went. Then I came to the ledge I'd been eyeing. It had a wide, thick lip that sloped upward and would give me cover, but right off I saw a problem.

From the ground it had appeared there was a solid trail of rock leading right up to that ledge. Only once I was up there, I could see it wasn't that way. The ledge was ten feet away, and almost fifteen feet higher than where I huddled. The way the rock was there, I was pretty sure I could make the climb, but I'd be hanging right out in the open the whole while.

I had to reach that ledge. From where I was, I couldn't quite see down into the wash, and worse, I was pretty much stuck. I was no kind of rock climber, but it was plain that the only way down from where I sat was to backtrack myself exactly. If I backed down, I figured there was a dead-certain chance one of those Indians would be waiting.

If I reached the ledge, I could work my way up and around, and find another way down.

First, though, I needed to know how bad I was hurt. Scooting down into cover as best I could, I looked myself over. I found the first damage while slipping off my gunbelt. The bullet had struck two of the cartridges in the loops on my belt.

Slipping my pants down a bit, I found the wound. After striking the cartridges in my belt, the bullet had turned sideways, striking my hipbone and glancing off. The gash it left wasn't more than three inches long but had bled freely, soaking my pants all the way to the knee.

How much damage it had done to the hipbone itself, there was no way of knowing. Not much, it seemed. Rolling up my bandanna, I crammed it right down into the wound, gritting my teeth and trying to curse at the same time.

I figured my pants and gunbelt would hold the bandanna in place, and when I pulled them up and tightened down the gunbelt, it seemed to work.

My rifle was also still usable, though I'd feared it wouldn't be. The bullet that had tore it from my hands had gone right through the stock, leaving a wide, splintered gap where it came out, but the action hadn't been hurt.

The sights were another story. The rifle had been dropped once, and knocked from my hands that second time, and it might be the sights were now out of line. They looked all right, but no man alive could tell by looking. Move the sights no more than a gnat's whisker, and you'd likely miss a man at a hundred yards.

The only way to tell was to take a shot at a mark, and that was the last thing I wanted to do right then.

My throat and chest felt raw from gasping for air, but it seemed I'd live a while . . . at least until one of those Zuni put another bullet in a place that counted for more than my hip.

Below me, I heard rifle fire. Most of it sounded like that old forty-four forty that Darby favored, but it sounded like a Henry was mixed in, and once I heard the unmistakable thundering boom of a heavy-caliber buffalo rifle.

The only thing certain was that I had to keep moving. Sitting where I was did me no good, and it sure as hell wasn't helping Darby.

My rifle was a problem. I couldn't make that climb one-handed, and I had no sling for the rifle. It came to me that I might toss it up first, but that was risky. It wasn't an easy toss, and even if I made it, I'd sure as hell knock those sights even more out of line than they might already be.

The shirt I was wearing was one of my favorites, but I ripped off one of the sleeves and made a sort of sling for the rifle. Slipping it over my shoulder, I took to climbing before I could change my mind.

I never felt so buck naked in my life. My shoulder blades wanted to scrunch together in expectation of the coming bullet, but I ignored the feeling and kept climbing. My hip hurt like blazes, but fear was the stronger force, and I made that climb in no more than three minutes.

I was just sliding onto the ledge when a bullet spanged off the rock inches from my hand, showering me with tiny pieces of rock. Not waiting to catch my breath, I eased up over that lip, rifle at the ready.

From there I could see right down into the wash. Right off

I saw the Zuni. He was ducking in and out of cover, taking potshots at Darby and the mules. A third mule was down.

Then I saw movement in the distance. When I looked that way I saw another damned Zuni had worked his way up in the rocks over yonder. He was even higher now, and out on the edge of that lip as I was, he had a clear shot at me. He was already drawing a bead.

I figured he had me sure. Then he quivered funny-like, and folded up like a rag doll. I heard the crack of Darby's rifle.

I reared up again, leveled my rifle down into the wash. The Indian down there had moved behind a clump of brush, and it took a minute to pick him up. When I did, it was just a flicker of movement. Taking careful aim, I levered three rounds through the brush. On the third shot, the Zuni leaped out, and even from the distance, I could see blood on his leg.

I had powder smoke drifting all around me, and he saw it plain. He brought his rifle in line, and we fired at the same time. His bullet cut through the collar of my shirt. Mine caught him in the center of the chest. He fell over backward, kicked a couple of times with his left foot, then was still.

That made three down. If we were right in our count, there should only be one more out there. But one was plenty. I was about to start working my way around to get higher, and move on to the other side of that rock tower, when I heard Darby yelling out.

"Hawkins, can you hear me?"

"I hear you."

"That fourth Injun took off. Best you hurry up and get back down here."

It took better than half an hour to work my way back down to level ground, and when I finally did, I was dead beat. I hobbled back to the wagon and found that Darby had already cut loose the dead mules and led the five others back behind the wagon.

"You looked chewed by a bear," he said.

"Feels like it."

"Like as not that Zuni was going for help. Best we be long gone before he gets it back here."

I nodded. "I reckon. You ain't got a bottle stashed anywhere, have you?"

"Wasn't sure you'd favor a man bringing whiskey along on the job."

"You got a bottle or not?"

"Hell, yes."

Darby reached under the sheets covering the freight and pulled a bottle of whiskey from a gap between two crates. He took a long drink, passed me the bottle. I took a drink to match his, then a second. "By God, that sits well."

Darby took a second drink, put the bottle back in its hiding place. "It do at that," he said. "That hole in you bad?"

"Guess I'll live. After we put some distance between us and those Zuni, I'll tend it proper."

We got the wagon hauled out, then hitched up the mules. We'd lost three, so we hitched four to the wagon and tied the spare along behind. (Fact is, six mules could haul that load without much trouble, and four could do it in a pinch, and that's why you run eight. If you lose a couple, you can still get where you're going.)

Once everything was set, we pushed on westward, driving those mules for all they were worth. We stopped a little earlier than need be to let the mules drink their fill and graze a spell, and while there I washed some of the blood off me.

My wound had stopped bleeding, but it was still ugly. We went ahead and made camp early enough to still have some daylight left, and right off Darby took a look at my wound.

He pulled the bandanna plug from the wound and

clucked his tongue like a mother hen. "By God, Hawkins," he said. "You're luckier than any man I ever knew."

"Lucky! How in hell do you figure that?"

"That bullet hadn't struck those ca'tridges afore it hit you," he said, "you'd be lying out there with a broken hip. Likely be dead before now."

"If I was lucky, that Indian would've missed altogether."

"If you weren't lucky, he'd have put that bullet through that mule head of yours. Now stay still. I'm going to have to stitch this closed, else it'll take a month to close up right. Or you'll get corruption in it. You ever see what gangrene does to a body?"

"I seen it. All right, you old bastard, go on ahead and stitch it up. Only dig out that bottle of whiskey first."

"Meant to. My throat's dry as sand."

Darby went to the wagon, dug out a needle and thread, brought it back along with the bottle of whiskey. He pulled the cork on the bottle and handed it to me. "Take a good, long drink," he said, "but save some. That's the only bottle I brought."

I took a good, long drink, winced at the burn of it. Darby took the bottle from me, and without warning, poured a big dollup right into my wound. I yelped and swore.

"You ready?" he asked.

"Hell, no, I ain't ready."

"Good. Here we go then."

"I said I ain't—"

Darby jabbed that long needle into the skin near the bullet wound. I don't know as I screamed, but I sure enough squealed. "Quit cher bellyachin'," Darby said. "I seen little boys take more pain. Some muleskinner you are."

"Muleskinner, my sweet arse," I said. "You lie down here and let me go to sewing on you. Then we'll see how loud you can yell."

"Hush up," Darby said, "else I'll sew this crooked. Two or three more and I'm finished."

It seemed more like two or three dozen more, but at last Darby slapped a clean bandage over his handiwork and leaned back. "That ought to hold you," he said. He took a long drink of whiskey, passed me the bottle.

"Not but one good drink left," he said.

He was right. I drained the bottle, sat up easy, testing to see how much my hip would take. It still hurt, mostly from those stitches pulling, but it was tolerable.

Picking up a stick from the fire, I lit a cigar, drew till it was going good. Easing over and getting my cup, I poured a cup of coffee, sipped at it. "I sure hope Billy's having an easier trip than we are," I said.

"No tellin'. Heading up that way, he probably won't be as likely to have Indian trouble, but there's plenty else to give a skinner hell."

"I reckon."

We ate, drank coffee, and talked till dark, then turned in. We moved our bedrolls so the wagon blocked us on one side and the mules on the other. For a time I lay awake listening to the night sounds. A coyote howled in the distance and was answered by another even farther away. A lonesomer sound I never heard. Pretty, but lonesome.

Something squealed close by . . . squealed the death of a small animal having the misfortune to run into a larger animal with big teeth and a bigger hunger. Then Darby's snoring drowned out everything else. A full moon swung across a star-filled sky, and for a time I watched it.

I'd wanted a place to ride free, and to rest my weary old bones. Instead I was lying in the middle of nowhere with an old man who snored louder than Gabriel's trumpet. On top of that, my hip still hurt.

"By God, Hawkins," I said softly. "You're dumber than a rock."

Rolling onto my good hip, I finally went to sleep. Seemed I hadn't no more than dropped off when Darby was shaking me awake.

"Be daylight in an hour," he said. "Might as well get on the trail early."

"I 'spect."

"Coffee's ready. Bacon and biscuits will be soon."

I nodded. My hip was stiff and began throbbing as soon as I sat up. My eyes felt full of grit, and my mouth tasted like old manure. I stood up, hobbled away from the wagons a piece, and emptied my bladder.

The morning air was cool, almost cold, but felt good. I lit the remains of a cigar and stood there a while, liking the feel of the fresh breeze in my face. By the time I walked back to the fire, breakfast was ready.

We ate the biscuits and bacon, and drank several cups of coffee without talking. When we finished, Darby cleaned the grease from the skillet with handfuls of sand, then began breaking camp.

It was full light by the time we were on the trail, and the day looked to be a hot one. So long as it was also peaceful, I didn't give a damn. Turned out it was. The only trouble we had the rest of the way to Patterson's was a broken stay chain, but we'd brought along spare links and fixed the chain in a matter of minutes.

We stayed at Patterson's long enough so he could unpack his things and see how much damage had been done. Two of those Indian bullets had made it through the crates, but the only damage was a small groove one bullet had cut in the underside of a fancy chair. Patterson waved it off when we offered to pay for the damage.

"After what you went through getting it here," he said, "I'd be a fool to complain about a scratch nobody will ever see."

We headed south then, and by the time we reached Globe I was done in. Without saying anything to anybody, I rode out to our ranch, stripped off my clothes, and dropped into bed. I didn't stir for ten hours.

CHAPTER 13

WHEN I FINALLY did wake up, it took me half an hour to get out of bed. Part of the reason it took so long was that the wound on my hip had stiffened up even more. Mostly, though, I was still tired. When I went out into the kitchen, there was nobody about.

After starting a fire in the cookstove and putting a pot of coffee on, I went out to the barn. The horses had all been put out to pasture. There was no telling how long they'd been out there, but there was enough graze to keep them fed a spell, and that little crick ran through the pasture, so they had food and water.

I forked a bunch of hay over the pasture fence just to keep them happy, then went back up to the house. Judging by the dust on the kitchen table, it didn't seem anybody had been around for a time.

Johnny should have been back from his fence-building trip long since. I couldn't say about Billy. I'd figured his run would be quicker than ours by a couple of weeks, but you just can't tell.

I ate a good breakfast, then went down to the crick and took a bath. I shaved, leaving the mustache this time, and put a fresh bandage on my hip.

There were chores needed doing about the place, and it was in my mind to ride over and see Kate, but I figured I ought to ride back into town first. I saddled Nugget and trotted off down the trail.

Helen Decker was the only one at the smithy; she was sitting in the freight office. When I stepped through the door, she gave as close to a smile as I ever saw on her face. "Good morning, Mr. Hawkins."

"Mornin', ma'am."

Looking about, I saw she'd fancied the office up a good bit. There were curtains on the window, a throw rug covered most of the floor, and some kind of pretty plant sat in the windowsill. And the office was spotlessy clean.

"This looks real fine, ma'am."

"Thank you, Mr. Hawkins. I was only trying to make it seem a little more . . . friendly."

"Yes, ma'am. Anybody about town?"

"Mr. Sullivan is somewhere around, I think."

"What about Billy and Johnny?"

"Mr. Martin is on a freight run out of Phoenix. Mr. Stevens was in town a couple of weeks ago. He also left for Phoenix. He said to tell you he was ready to trap the horses and not to expect him back for three or four weeks."

"All right. Sounds like everything is going about like he wanted. But, ma'am, you need to get in the habit of calling us all by our first names, else we won't recognize ourselves."

"I suppose I could do that."

"Good. All right if we call you Helen?"

This time she did smile. "Certainly. I'd like that."

"Fine, Helen. We're all set then. I'm going to look around and see if I can find Darby."

As I started back out the door, she stopped me. "Mr. Hawkins . . . I mean, Benjamin, may we have a talk?"

"Plain Ben will do. About what?"

"The business here."

"Can it wait awhile? Till after lunch? Say two, or so?"

"Of course."

"Fine."

Walking on out, I started down to O'Brien's. Marshal Reynolds was just coming down the street, and we talked awhile. He said Hoag Willis had struck again, this time killing a rancher and stealing two hundred head of cattle. He'd made it down across the border before the cavalry could catch up, and that was that.

I went on down to O'Brien's then. Dunie yelled out a hello and drew me a beer. I took it gratefully.

"How'd your run to Santa Fe go?"

I drank half the beer in three long swallows. "I've earned easier money," I said. "Maybe not as much, but sure as hell easier."

"I'll stick to tending bar. I make enough to keep up, and even put a bit in the bank now and then. No, sir. You'll not catch me out running freight through Apache country."

"Can't say I blame you any. I'd open my own saloon, 'cept I'd likely drink myself right out of business."

"I've seen it happen."

"Darby been in?"

"Not today. Wait a minute. Is that him coming in? Naw, can't be."

I turned around just as Darby came through the doors. He was clean shaven and wore a suit and, by God, a derby hat. He was drenched in some kind of fancy-smelling barber goop.

"What are you all done-up for," I asked. "Somebody die?"

"Whatta you mean by that? Can't a man change his clothes without somebody croaking?"

"Didn't think you could," I said.

"It jest so happens I'm taking Miss Decker to lunch. Anything wrong with that?"

"I don't think I know anybody by that name," Dunie said. "She work at one of the saloons?"

Darby's face reddened. "Hell, no, she don't work at a saloon. She's a lady."

"She works for me," I said. "By God, Darby, I knew you took a fancy to her, but I didn't know it was enough to make you take a bath and dress up like a dandy."

"A man's got to get cleaned up once in a while, don't he? I don't know what you're makin' such a fuss about."

"Now, don't take it that way," Dunie said. "We were just funning you. Have a beer. It's on the house."

"Well, I guess so. Why not? I can't have more'n one, though. I'd not want Miss Decker to think I'm a drunk."

Dunie and I looked at each other and shook our heads a little. "By God," I said. "Now I heard it all."

Me and Darby found a table to sit at while we drank our beers. Dunie was having a slow day, and after a bit he came over and joined us. As men will, we took turns telling tales, talking about things we'd done and seen. First thing I knew, I looked up and it was high noon.

Darby had stuck to his guns and hadn't drank but the one beer. Now he stood up and took off, saying he was supposed to be at Molly's no later than noon. I'd had three beers, but still felt dry.

I was feeling restless, but couldn't put no reason on why. I thought about drinking another beer, decided against it.

I couldn't rightly say what was bothering me. I hadn't been back off the trail a full day yet, but the urge to get out and ride, to get away, was on me strong.

It was a feeling I'd felt often enough, though never when sitting in a saloon, drinking beer. Generally, such an urge hit after I'd spent a long winter in a line shack. Sometimes when I was on a cattle drive and had been doing the same damned thing day after day.

Most times I chalked it up to cabin fever and let it go at that. Other times I admitted it was something else. Like Johnny, I'd been a traveling man much of my life, always looking to see what was over the next hill, beyond the blue horizon. I never could rightly say what I was looking for, but it was sure as hell something I'd never found. Beneath it all, I always believed there'd be something at the end of the yondering, that one day I'd say, "Here it is. This is what I've been looking to find."

When I saw that land out there around the Mogollon Plateau, I'd thought sure I'd found the spot. Then why the sudden restlessness? Why the urge to get up, straddle Nugget, and ride like hell?

Was it just to feel the wind on my face? Just the need to ride alone and free as far away from other folks as I could get?

I allowed it wasn't. It was like a hollow spot way down inside. That land out yonder seemed to slide down in there and fill most of it, but not all. Some part of that hollow still needed filling, and I'll be damned if I could figure out why and with what.

Hell, maybe that land out there was enough . . . or would be once I owned my share proper. Once I'd built a house and had a porch to sit on where I might watch the sun go down, maybe that would still the urge to move?

Right in the middle of thinking about that, another thought came to me. "Dunie, you ever get any ranchers in here?"

Dunie shrugged his big shoulders. "Now and again. There aren't many ranchers in the area yet. Those that do get into Globe seem to drink over at the Longhorn. Guess the name of the place appeals to them. Fact is, there's so many copper miners around Globe, I've been thinking hard about calling this place 'The Copper Mine.' "

"You have any idea where a man could buy himself a pony? A small one, fit for a kid?"

"No, sir, I surely wouldn't. You wanting it for the Smalley boy?"

I nodded. "Promised him one some time back, only I've been busier than a one-legged man in a butt-kicking contest. Seems like I ought to get to it."

"I'd say so."

"Dunie, can I ask you a question?"

"You can ask anything. No promises that I'll answer."

"You ever been married?"

Dunie took a long drink of beer. "No, sir. There was a time when I thought I would be. That was a long time ago, and a long way from here. Back in Boston."

"What happened?"

"Nothing, really. My feet started itching, and the only way to scratch them seemed to be by walking. So one day I went to walking. Next thing I knew the Mississippi was behind me, and I never crossed back over.

"Now, well, I run a two-by-twice saloon with an upstairs full of whores. Don't know as I'd want any woman who would have me."

"You ever regret it—leaving Boston, I mean?"

"Ah, hell, I don't know. Her name was Mary, and she had a face like an angel. At least, that's how I remember her. But I knew if I married her I'd never see anything beyond Boston. I'd have six kids, and I'd die working at some nothing job her father gave me.

"Do I regret leaving? Sometimes I do, Hawkins. Usually on nights when I've had too much to drink . . . But those times are just foolish thoughts, and I know it. I chose the life I'm living, Hawkins, and the larger part of the time, I'm happy with it."

Dunie grinned, drained the last of the beer from his glass. "Besides, Hawkins, I've been a lot of places and done a lot of things. I don't expect to run this saloon forever.

"There's still places I haven't seen . . . hell, it's been in my mind to cross the ocean and see the old country. Who knows, maybe one morning I'll wake up, sell everything I own, and head for the nearest ocean."

"Ireland, you mean? You've never been there?"

"No. My parents were no more than youngsters themselves when they left. I was born in New York. We moved to Boston when I was fifteen. What about you, Hawkins? Why didn't you ever marry and settle down?"

"Never had the chance, I guess. I've always been a hard man. Never made no money. Never had no truck with decent women."

"Seems like you're on the right track now."

I shrugged. "Right now it just seems like more hard work. I'm making better money, but you want to know the truth? My feet are starting to itch something awful."

"You planning to walk away?"

"I don't know, Dunie. I honest to God don't know."

"It might be you're not looking far enough ahead. Maybe you're looking down at the tracks, instead of at the light at the end of the tunnel."

"Could be. Only with my luck, I can't see the light on account of the train bearing down on me. I want that land out yonder, Dunie. I never wanted anything as bad in my whole life. Guess maybe I have the feeling I'm butting my head against a stone wall. That's all it really is.

"I've never been one to give up, and when you get down to it, I don't guess I will this time. I just ain't sure I'm smart enough to pull this off."

"Don't sell yourself short, Hawkins. Always seemed to me the smart man is the one who works the hardest. Luck, now that's a different horse. But even there, a man who's up and doing seems to have more luck than a man who sits around waiting for luck to come to him."

"Maybe you're right, Dunie. Maybe you're right. Well, hell. I'm not getting anything done sitting here on my arse. Guess I'll go see if I can find a good pony."

After I left O'Brien's, I hit half a dozen other saloons, and even the livery down at the other end of town, but had no luck anywhere. The bartender down at the Longhorn did tell me to come back along about nightfall when a couple of ranchers sometimes drifted in.

By then it was near two, and time to see Helen Decker. I walked back to the smithy, and found Helen sitting at the small desk in the office. I dropped into the chair where customers usually sat. "You wanted to talk?" I said.

"Yes, but after thinking about it, well, perhaps it isn't my place to say what I've been thinking."

"You go on ahead, Helen. I won't bite."

"Very well," she said hesitantly. "But if you think I'm out of line, please stop me. I won't be insulted."

"That's fair."

"Well, I know you only hired me to keep the books in order, and to be here when no one else is around, but in keeping the books, in adding the columns of numbers, and in looking at the freight orders, you can't help but see things, Mr. Ha . . . I mean, Ben."

"Such as what?"

"Profits, loss, projected income, operating expenses. That sort of thing."

"Yes, ma'am. What's your point?"

"It's only that Mr. Sullivan and I, well, we've had lunch together a couple of times now. He's told me what you and the others are working for, including how much money you need, and when you need it."

"That's no secret. He had the right to tell you."

"Yes. I didn't mean that. But as I said, in keeping the books . . . May I speak frankly?"

"Wouldn't do any good to talk otherwise."

She bobbed her head. "Yes. Very true. I understand Mr. Stevens, Johnny, believes he may earn three thousand dollars or so from his current venture?"

"Catching those mustangs, you mean? That's what he expects. Give or take a bit."

"You aren't going to make it, Ben. Going as you are, you won't earn enough money. Not even if Johnny does earn three thousand dollars."

That made me sit up and pay attention. "You can tell that just by those books? Are you certain sure?"

"I am. The problem is time. You have two wagons, and each freight run requires a certain amount of time. Mr. Sullivan went through the list of runs you have waiting, and told me how long each would take, along with the probable profit.

"You have only two months remaining, and even if every

run goes perfectly, and even if Johnny does succeed in bringing in three thousand dollars, you'll still be somewhere around twenty-five hundred dollars short at the end of two months.

"That's the very best you can expect. If there are unexpected losses, or unexpected delays in delivering any freight, you'll be in even worse shape."

My mouth felt dry. "I'll ask you again, Helen. Are you absolutely certain sure?"

"Yes. It's really no more than adding numbers. The way you are going now, you have no chance of making ten thousand dollars in so short a time. No chance at all."

"Can you go through the numbers with me? Run through everything so I can understand?"

"Certainly."

Moving my chair around to where I could see the books, we went through them. Then we went through the list of runs we had waiting, and everything else.

She was right as rain, and no doubt about it. The way we were going, we were going to come up short. Maybe a lot short.

CHAPTER 14

WE WENT OVER the numbers again, and came up with the exact same answer. I wanted to cuss. I wanted to stomp around, cuss a blue streak, then get drunk. I held off on the cussing on account of Helen being there, but biting off those words wasn't the easiest thing I ever did.

"If you could find a buyer in time," Helen said, "you might make up the difference by selling the freight line right before the deadline."

"Yes, ma'am, we might. But we'll need the money this place brings in. Won't do us much good to get that land out yonder if we can't pay the mortgage.

"I don't know what we'll do out there. Run some horses, likely some cattle, but it'll take at least a couple of years to make it all pay for itself. Maybe four or five years. Until it does, we'll still have to pay the bank its due."

If we went to hunting wild horses full-time, we might cut out enough young stuff to start our own herd and still sell enough to make the payments we owed. But that was iffy. Real iffy. Hunting wild horses was always a hit-or-miss affair. There was money to be made in it, but sometimes months went by between finding a good herd, catching enough to matter, and selling them for a good profit.

The way Johnny was going about it couldn't be done often . . . if it worked this time.

Johnny was the expert on mustangs, and if he said he could make this work, I'd believe him until shown otherwise. But that didn't mean any of us would ever come across a situation where we could pull the same trick again.

Still, it might be possible. I'd thought to ask about the

mortgage payments on the land, and rounding it off, they came in at just a hair over two hundred dollars a month. Most folks, ranchers, anyway, paid the bank twice a year, and sometimes only once a year.

And very damn few paid ahead, meaning they were a full year behind when they sold cattle and settled up. That was the main reason a hard winter could wipe out a rancher. Bankers were mostly understanding about the way a rancher had to wait till he drove cattle to market before paying his bills, but they also understood that it took years to rebuild should a man lose the better part of his herd.

So if a man missed that yearly catch-up, the bank didn't generally give him a second chance.

That's what I figured would happen with us if we didn't have a good source of money coming in outside the ranch we wanted.

There would be times when we could make enough to pay on that mortgage without any trouble, and other times when we wouldn't have two nickels to rub together. It was those times I worried about.

"You got anything there to show how much we make off the smithy?"

"In profit? Not really. I'm afraid you didn't keep very good records until now. But from the receipts, I'd say something like eighty dollars per month."

Eighty a month. That was better than I figured. We could likely up that to a hundred or so by working at it full-time. We might even get up to a hundred and forty.

But that would be working from can-see to can't-see six or seven days a week. Working like that, we'd have no chance to do anything with the land, even if we got it.

"Helen," I said, "I'm sure open to ideas, if you have any, but I don't think selling the freight business would work. Not yet, anyway."

If we could raise enough to get that land, and then sell,

well, that'd be different. Then we could use the money to pay a year or two ahead at the bank. But if we sold the business just to make that up-front payment, we'd have no way at all to pay on the mortgage.

"What about wagons?" I asked her. "I don't know if we could get another wagon or two up and running in time to help, but if we could, would that do it?"

We spent another hour running through the numbers. Experienced muleskinners were hard to come by, and they wanted good wages. Right then, what with the Apache trouble and all the outlaws about, I couldn't expect to hire an experienced man for less than twenty-five dollars a week, and that kind of money added up fast.

And it would likely cost even more to find men willing to take a wagon out alone. Swampers were easier to find, but even a swamper would likely ask twelve or fifteen dollars a week. Even that was a good bit of cash. Then again, once the wagon and new string of mules were paid for, the profits would more than offset the wages.

My biggest worry was the same as Murphy's. If the Apache trouble should end, or another freighter move into the area, we'd have to cut our prices by half. I'd pay hell earning enough to buy that land then.

Me and Helen went up one side of the numbers and down the other. I wasn't much on figuring, and it took me long minutes of thought to add what seemed to jump from her head in no time at all. But she led me along and never went ahead till I'd caught up, so we got there together.

Finally we had the numbers all added up and in pretty rows. If we added another wagon, we might make it. It would be cutting things close, but we just might make it.

If we didn't have any big, unexpected losses, if the Apache and outlaws let us keep our prices up, and if no other freighters moved in on us.

First we'd have to find the right deal on a wagon and more mules. And we'd have to hurry. Me and Helen figured a third wagon would have to run for five weeks to make up the difference, which meant we had three weeks to find one, make a deal, and hire men to drive it. Not much time.

Finally I stood up, stretched my back. We'd been at those books and the thinking a good three hours. And by God, if that wasn't the hardest work I'd ever done. By the time we finished, I felt like I'd made three runs to Santa Fe and back.

About the time I thought we were finished, Darby came in. He asked what we'd been up to, and I laid it out for him. "It ain't more wagons we need," he said, "it's bigger wagons. Like those caravan wagons of Murphy's."

"You know where we can tie into some cheap?"

"Not specifically. But if that's what you want, the best place to find 'em is always Santa Fe. There's freighters there a-plenty, mostly running east and north, and a body can always find a wagon at a fair price. We already got plenty of mules. Not to say it wouldn't cost some. How cheap were you thinking?"

I thought a minute. Between what I had left from buying the wagons and mules off Mrs. Richardson, and what we'd earned at the smithy and on the Santa Fe run, I was holding almost two thousand dollars.

"When's Billy due back?"

"He had a pretty short run," Darby said. "Day after to-morrow. No later than the day after that."

"How much is he supposed to make?"

"He's doing a two-way run. Helen, you got it wrote down, don't you?"

Helen went through a small ledger. "Yes, here it is. After expenses, he should make about five hundred dollars."

"Bueno. Darby, what could you get in Santa Fe for a thousand dollars?"

"A couple of old wagons or maybe one new one. Might do a little better or a little worse, depending on what's to be had. Throw in another two hundred and I could likely do a good bit better."

"How long would it take you?"

"If I pushed hard there and back, and found a deal quick? Not less'n three weeks. Maybe four. Mostly that's travel time. I might find a wagon and enough mules to bring them back the first day. Might take two weeks. No tellin'."

"Damn. There ain't no place closer a man can buy a couple of those big wagons?"

"Might be, but not that I know about. I can ask around."

I didn't see any other way. "You ask around," I said. "But if you don't come up with something by the time Billy gets back, I'm going to send you to Santa Fe."

"Jest me?"

"Can't you handle it alone?"

"Hell . . . sorry, Helen. O' course I can handle it alone. I ain't no child. But there ain't many as would trust someone to ride off alone with enough money to tempt a preacher."

"You planning on stealing it?"

"I ain't never stole nothing in my life . . . 'ceptin' a horse one time. But I figure it was owed to me."

"Then why shouldn't I trust you?"

"Godda . . . hell . . . sorry, Helen. There ain't no reason you shouldn't trust me. But what if I was to be robbed, or had some such hard luck?"

"That could happen to me as well as you. Do you want to go buy us a wagon and mules, or not?"

"Shore I wanna go."

"Then it's settled. If we can't find something closer by Friday, you'll head for Santa Fe on Saturday. Might be you ought to take the stage there."

"By God, I hadn't thought of that. The Butterfield would take a week off the trip. Maybe a bit more. I'd still have to drive the wagon back, but it sure would cut down on the up-front time."

"A week could make the difference. Now, I've had it for today. Helen, is there any reason we can't put off more runs until Billy gets back?"

"No. You shouldn't miss too many days, but I don't suppose two will mean much."

"Good. In that case, I'm going to have supper, and then I'm going to see if I can find a pony. Either of you hungry? It's on me."

They looked at each other, and some kind of signal I didn't see must have passed between them. They said no at exactly the same time, and Helen blushed a little. "Thank you," she said, "but I promised Mr. Sullivan, er, Darby, that I would prepare him supper tonight. You're welcome to join us, of course."

"No, you two run on along. I'll close up, then walk on down to Molly's."

"If you're sure," Helen said. "You really are welcome to join us."

"Thanks, but if you don't mind, I'll take a rain check. You two run on along. I'll close things down."

Helen put away the books. Then she and Darby left.

After making sure everything was shut down tight, I did the same.

My pa used to tell me there'd be good days and bad days. Any fool could handle the good days, he said. The mark of a man was how well he handled the bad ones.

I'd had my share of bad days . . . enough to know they came in a variety of shapes and sizes. Back during the war, near all the days had been bad. But the thing that surprised me was that the days you'd expect to be the worst most often weren't.

The days when the drums began beating and the cannon began thundering were bad, all right. There just wasn't anything pleasant about marching into waiting guns and seeing friends torn apart, left lying bloody and dying on the field until the fighting was over.

It ripped a man's soul to count the dead, and to listen to the screams coming from the surgeon's tents. And there was always that little quiver in your gut that came from knowing you might be the next to die or the next to lose a leg, an arm, or an eye.

But those weren't the worst days. Seeing friends killed around you, rushing into battle while screaming your lungs out to keep up your courage, that was a time when the mind kind of shut itself down and you just made it through the best way you could.

No, sir. The worst days during the war always came between battles. It was then, most often around the fire at night, when you finally realized those friends really were gone. You'd turn to say something to a face that had been there from the start, and now it was gone, replaced by some young kid who had no better sense than to leave home just so he could die a whole lot sooner.

It was there, in the cold of the night, with dysentery rumbling your guts, and the knowing in your head that however the war turned out it wasn't worth all the dying and killing . . . that's when it all piled up and you wanted to run away, but of course you didn't.

I don't know as any of us stayed because we were brave. Mostly we stayed because we were afraid. Afraid of what folks would think if we ran, and afraid that once we started running, we would never stop.

Suddenly, it seemed to me now that I'd been running ever since the war ended. The name I put to it was restlessness, but it was running all the same.

Maybe we wouldn't make it here. Maybe we'd break our backs trying, and still lose out on that land. But as I walked down to Molly's I decided I wasn't going to run no more. Right here I'd make my stand, and if I lost, well, hell, what if I did?

I'd gone near my whole life with nothing more than a month's wages in my pocket, and that only until I could find the nearest saloon. I'd once heard a man say he spent near all his money on cheap whiskey and cheaper women, and the rest of it he wasted.

Guess I took that to heart. Sure as hell, I'd gone through plenty of both in my time.

But, goddamnit, I was way the hell too old to spend any more time sowing wild oats. The last time I'd been to the barber, he swung me around and let me look in the mirror at the job he'd done. He'd cut my hair just fine, but that wasn't what I noticed first.

First thing I noticed was a tired old man staring right at me. It took a minute to realize that the tired old man I saw was my own reflection.

I just didn't have many more tries in me. If I didn't get my piece of that land out there now, I doubted I ever would. I'd spend the rest of my days pounding iron at the smithy, or maybe hauling freight, and when I was too old to do either, hell, who knew what would come then?

At the same time, I knew somewhere deep down inside that it wasn't so much the land I wanted, as what that land represented. It was a way of saying I'd done something, had something to leave behind me.

But whatever it was, I decided I was making my stand. I was going to own that land, or die in the trying.

By God, I wanted to get drunk. I wanted to get drunk and stay drunk for a week.

Instead I sat there at Molly's and ate supper without even tasting what was on my plate. Then I got up and went looking for a pony. It took some doing, but I finally came across a man who said he had a little pinto that ought to do the trick.

The man's name was Hiram Wallace, and he lived about six miles west and a little north of Globe. He made his living raising hogs, and from his account, there were plenty of buyers about.

"Folks can get salt pork and bacon," he said, "but fresh

ham is another story. If there's anyone else in this whole damned territory raising hogs, I ain't met them."

He had a point. I told him I'd ride out to his place come morning and take a look at the pinto, then I bought him a drink. After that he bought me one, and pretty soon the only worry I had was could I walk over to the smithy without falling on my face.

I made it, and there I crawled up into the loft and went to sleep in the hay.

CHAPTER 15

I DON'T KNOW if it was the drinking, the sleep, or just the fine morning air, but when I woke up at dawn I felt better than I had in weeks.

The trace of a mild hangover was there, but I washed it away at the horse trough and stood there enjoying the morning.

After cleaning up proper, I started down to Molly's. I passed Helen along the way, and we said good morning. Once at Molly's, I ate a healthy breakfast, smoked a cigar, and sat there drinking coffee.

Marshal Reynolds came in. He looked haggard. He saw me, came over, and sat down.

"Don't often see you out this early," I said. "Have a bad night?"

He rubbed his hand across his face, nodded. "Hard night and a hard morning is more like it. Though I guess Mrs. Reynolds had the hardest. She's expecting, and mornings have been hard on her. Today was worse than usual.

"Last night it was her back giving her fits, and this morning she couldn't tolerate the smell of food, so I thought it best to come down here."

"This one your first?"

"Yes, sir. We've wanted children since we first got married, only it never took. This time it did, I guess. We're sure looking forward to it, but I never thought about it being this hard on Mrs. Reynolds."

I sat and drank more coffee while Marshal Reynolds ate

his breakfast. Once he was through, he pulled out a pack of Cross Cuts and offered me one.

I'd never smoked cigarettes much. Never had the hands to roll them proper. So mostly I smoked cigars and found pleasure in doing so. But I'd been in the drugstore to get myself some aloe pills on account of being bound up one time, and I went so far as to buy some ready-mades.

Never got to try them out, though. Don't know if they fell out of my pocket, or if I laid them somewhere and didn't pick them up. Whichever happened, I never smoked one. I'd meant to buy more and just never had.

I took the one that Marshal Reynolds offered, lit it, drew the smoke in deep . . . and went right into a hard coughing fit.

"They take some getting used to," he said. "Sure go well after eating or with a cup of coffee, though."

I finished the cigarette, and it wasn't bad after the coughing stopped.

Finally I stood up. "Well, I have some riding to do this morning," I said. "Best get to it. Give my best to Mrs. Reynolds. See you later, Marshal."

Going on down to the smithy, I went into the office. Helen was there, and so was Darby. I told them where I was headed. "Shouldn't take me long."

"There's already been folks in asking about work they left at the smithy," Darby said.

"They can wait till tomorrow. Guess I'll have to put in a full day. I came to Globe to start a smithy, and now it's getting to be more trouble than it's worth.

"I'd thought to hire an extra driver so either me or Billy could be here working the smithy full-time, only it ain't going to work. The way wages are, I'd have to pay a man as much as we make from the smithy."

"I don't see any way around it," Darby said. "Might come to closing the smithy . . . to general folks, leastways."

I thought about it a minute. "Not unless we have to. Guess we'll keep working it catch as catch can, and hope folks don't get in too much of an uproar when we're late getting to their work."

"I reckon most folks are patient. 'Specially since this is the only smithy in town. Those that ain't can be hanged."

"Reckon that's what it comes down to. You doing anything to look for a wagon yet?"

Darby pointed to a stack of newspapers. "Been going through those. No luck so fur. Had the time, I'd ride over to Phoenix, but that's a long piece.

"I might pick up a wagon from one of the copper mines . . . the bigger mines run a few supply wagons of their own. Ain't likely, though. Those wagons don't come cheap, and the mine folks generally hang onto them until they ain't worth using or fixin'.

"It looks like you're going to Santa Fe."

"That's how the stick's floatin' right now."

I went on out and saddled Nugget. Stopping by O'Brien's, I bought a bottle of the best whiskey he had, thinking it might help me make a deal. With that tucked into my saddlebag, I rode out of town.

Hiram Wallace had told me how to find his place, but the directions hadn't been exactly the kind to give confidence. He'd said I should ride along the road four or five miles, and cut off north when I came to a formation of rock where three horse-sized boulders sat side by side.

Once there, he claimed I'd find a trail his wagon wheels had cut through the hills. Just follow that, he said, and I'd have no trouble.

He was right about that, only I found three different spots where boulders sat side by side, and a fourth where they weren't lined up so well. The fourth was the only group near a trail of any kind.

Finding nothing else, I followed the trail for two miles or so, and finally came up to a house built of adobe. A roofed porch had been added, and there in a chair sat Hiram Wallace.

When I rode up closer, he looked up and grinned. "See you found the place."

"No trouble at all."

"Tie your horse yonder and sit a spell."

He had a hitching post twenty yards out from the house, and I looped Nugget's reins around it, pulled the bottle from my saddlebag, and walked over to the porch. "By God," he said, "I like a man who brings his own bottle."

"Thought maybe you'd be feeling kind of dry by now."

"I am at that. Sit yourself down." He twisted in his chair and yelled through the open door of the house. "Sally May, bring us a couple of cups on out here."

I heard some rattling around, then a woman stepped through the door and onto the porch. She wore a plain cotton dress, her black hair in a ponytail. She gave me a timid grin, handed her husband a pair of tin cups, and disappeared back into the hollow darkness.

He looked at the bottle before opening it. "That cost more than I can afford to pay," he said. "Let's see how it tastes."

He opened the bottle, poured both cups half full, handed me one. We took a drink, looked at each other. "That goes down real well, don't it?" he said.

"Better than rotgut by a sight."

A couple of kids came tearing out of the house, raced across the porch, then around the corner. A toddler came following, a bit unsteady on his feet, but trying his best to follow.

We sat there and talked for a spell, then Wallace poured a bit more whiskey into each of our cups. "Guess you'll be wanting to see that pinto? We may as well go have a look."

"Where is he?"

"Got a corral around behind the house and back a bit."

Wallace had built his house about as far from other folks as a man could get without going out into the mountains. "Don't you worry about Apaches out here?" I asked.

"Don't fret a bit. Might, but I know most of them personal. I worked for a time as an Indian agent. Likely I was the only honest one they ever met.

"Breaking off the reservation won't do none of them any good, but I sure as hell don't blame them. It's a miserable life they're living out there. Especially for those old enough to remember how things used to be."

The pinto was chomping on a mouthful of hay when we stepped up to the corral. It was a pretty thing, maybe a little bigger than I'd planned, but not too big. It was the kind of horse a man could ride, so long as he didn't plan on throwing a rope over a big bull.

"How old is he?"

"Five, almost six. Rightly speaking, he belongs to my oldest boy, and you'll have to dicker price with him."

"Why's he wantin' to sell?"

"Bobby's fifteen, and he's feeling his oats. That pinto would do him for years to come, but you know how growing kids are. He figures he's full grown, and he wants a horse to match. Outside of the pinto, I have two horses for the wagon, and two broke to saddle, and I need them all. If I could, I'd buy the boy a horse, but cash is tight."

"I heard you were selling hogs faster than you could raise them."

"That's a fact. But I'm not raising all that many yet, and I have to keep rolling the money back into the place. Besides, I've damn near lost count of how many kids we have, and I can't train none of them to go without food and clothes."

"Never had that problem, but I can see how you could spend a lot of money that way. Where's the boy? Bobby, you said?"

"That's right. Robert Jackson Wallace, to give his full name. He's out hunting somewhere. I told him to be back by noon, and he's usually good about getting back when told."

I glanced up at the sun. "Looks close to that now."

Wallace pulled out his watch. "A few minutes after. You hungry?"

"I could eat a bite."

"Sally May ought to have a stew ready by now. Let's go fill our stomachs. Likely Bobby will be back before we finish."

We went back to the house and I met Sally May proper. And all the Wallace kids except Bobby. There were six of them, running from not much over a year, up to about nine. Once they started in on lunch, I could see what Wallace meant about keeping them fed.

We ate, then went back out to the porch, carrying coffee in our cups this time. I lit a cigar, offered one to Wallace. We lit up, sat smoking and drinking coffee. Twenty minutes later, Bobby Wallace showed up. He came out of the brush dragging a fair-sized mule deer behind him.

"Sorry about getting back late, Pa. I had that buck in my sights three times before I got a shot. Then I had to gut him out before starting back."

"The meat will go good," Wallace said, "but you shouldn't keep a man waiting."

"No harm done on my account," I said. "That's a fine buck."

"Thanks."

"Your pa tells me you're looking to get yourself a man-sized horse. You in a swapping mood?"

"Didn't think I could get much of a horse in trade for the pinto. Not as good as I want, anyway. Figured I'd have to sell him, and save the rest."

"I ain't saying I don't have money," I said, "and if you want, we'll dicker it out that way. Only I have more horses than I rightly need, and I'm trying to save money myself."

"I'd be willing to look at what you got."

"We'll have to ride back into Globe. Maybe out to a place we have south a piece, if there's nothing in Globe you like."

"Can I go, Pa?"

"Don't see why not. Get back soon as you can."

I waited until Bobby and his pa hung the buck on a skinning post and Bobby saddled the pinto. I thanked Sally May for the lunch, and we rode off toward Globe.

Once there, I trotted the spare horses out into the corral where Bobby could see them proper.

"You can take your pick," I said, "and we'll trade even."

"Does that include the buttermilk?"

"Sure."

"That's the one I want."

He'd picked the best of the lot right off. That buttermilk wasn't more than four years old and would sell for a hundred and fifty or better. "Where'd you learn so much about horses?"

"Some from the Apaches, the rest from the cavalry. When my pa worked on the reservation, I spent about half my time at the fort and the rest out with the Apaches."

"That's the best way to learn. You in the mood to trade saddles? I have one in the shop there that's made for roping. It's six or seven years old, but that's young for a good saddle."

We made the trade, and Bobby tossed a loop over the buttermilk, then saddled it. He stepped up into the saddle, a pleased look on his face. "I guess I shouldn't complain," he said, "but it seems to me you're taking a big loss. That pinto of mine isn't worth half this one, and that's not even considering the saddle."

"Depends on how you look at it. I don't need the buttermilk, but I know someone who does need the pinto."

"Well, I sure do thank you. But my pa is never going to believe I traded even."

"Just tell him you slick-talked me."

"He sure won't believe that. Well, guess I'd better be getting back. By the way, the pinto answers to the name of Star. I gave him the name because of the way that white on his forehead is shaped."

"It's a fitting name."

He trotted that buttermilk down the street, sitting up ramrod straight and peacock proud.

Darby had been watching us. Once Bobby rode off, he shook his head. "By God, Hawkins, you near gave that boy the horse."

"He'll make good use of it, I suspect. There anything I'm needed for around here?"

"Not if you ain't workin' today. Better if you ain't around, in fact. That way we can tell folks the boss is gone, and they should come back tomorrow."

"Sounds right by me. I'll be out to Kate's, or at the ranch, if you all need me. Might be back tonight, an' might not. Morning for sure."

"All right."

I had a present for Todd, and thinking to get everybody in on the picture, I walked about town looking for something fitting to buy Kate and Laura. I'd never bought for a woman in my life, but I got some help from a woman in a dress shop.

They had all kinds of things besides clothes, and once I explained the situation, that woman didn't think more'n a minute before leading me over to a table covered with things I'd never have thought of on my own.

She suggested a fancy music box for Kate, and a comb, brush, and mirror set for Laura. Feeling like a fish out of water, I went with her ideas.

With those things wrapped pretty. I made a couple of more stops, buying candy, coffee, flour and sugar, plus half a dozen packs of those Cross Cuts for myself.

Tying those things to the pinto's saddle, I climbed back on Nugget, scooped up the pinto's reins, and started out of town at an easy trot. When I rode within shouting distance of Kate's, she was just calling Todd and Laura in for supper.

CHAPTER 16

LAURA WAS WALKING back from the barn, Todd running full tilt. Laura waved her hand over her head and kept walking toward the house. When Todd saw me he never slowed down, but simply cut and continued his run straight toward me.

I stopped long enough to scoop him up into the saddle with me. His eyes were on the pinto behind me, but I think he was afraid to ask the question on his mind. We rode up to the house, and I eased him down to the ground.

Kate stood there with her hands on her hips, holding a dish towel in her left. Her hair was loose, and a line of flour marked one cheek. She wore a green dress, and she was almighty fetching.

"I was beginning to think you'd left the country," she said.

"Came close enough. Been to Santa Fe, and took the long route back."

I dropped to the ground, took the big sack off the pinto, then handed the reins to Todd. "Think you're big enough to handle him?"

Todd's eyes widened to the size of silver dollars, and he let out a little squeal. "He's mine? He's really mine?"

"Yes, sir, he surely is. You ever rode a horse on your own?"

"Yes, sir. My daddy taught me. Yes, sir. I sure have."

"Can you get into the saddle?"

Todd wasn't tall enough to get his foot into the stirrup, but before I could help, he jumped up, grabbed ahold of the pommel, and crawled right up the side of the pinto.

"Hang on a minute," I said, "and I'll shorten the stirrups to fit."

It didn't take but a minute to get the stirrups shortened so his feet reached. That done, he wheeled the pinto around and trotted toward the barn. I walked up onto the porch next to Kate, and together we watched Todd trot here and there.

"It was wonderful of you to buy him a pony," she said, "but are you sure it's safe?"

"It's gentle as any lamb," I said. "There's always the chance of gettin' throwed, but he seems to know what he's doing. And most boys are riding long before they're Todd's age. I'd allow Laura wasn't much older."

"No, I guess she wasn't. It really was wonderful of you, Ben. My problem now is how to get him off the horse and inside the house for dinner."

"Tell him I brung along some candy. That might help."

"A pony of his own and candy too."

"Yes, ma'am," I said. "And that ain't all. Guess I brung along something for you and Laura, too."

"For me? What on earth? Oh, what is it?"

"Let's go inside. If you got one of those pies baked, I might show you what I brung."

It took a couple of minutes, but Kate finally got Todd down off Star, and we went inside. First thing I did was unload the coffee, sugar, and flour.

"Seemed like we all eat over here so often, I ought to give something back. And I brought these."

I gave each of them the things I'd bought, and Laura began tearing at the wrappings. She got it undone, saw what was inside. She smiled wide, bounced on her feet, and hugged me. "Oh, Ben, thank you. I've been wanting these very things, but we couldn't afford them."

She gave me a peck on the cheek, and I blushed all the way to my heels. "Guess I just got repaid a hundred times over."

Kate hesitated a minute. "My mother told me to beware

a man who came bearing gifts," she said. "She said it was sometimes a way of saying hello, and sometimes a way of saying goodbye. You aren't leaving us, are you, Ben?"

"Not for a spell. I need to get back to town by morning."

"That's not what I meant. I mean, you aren't thinking about leaving for good?"

Somehow, it suddenly felt hotter inside the house. Hot enough to make me sweat. "No. I'm not going anywhere, Kate."

"Good."

She unwrapped the music box, and the look on her face was one I couldn't read. She rubbed her hand over the smooth finish, opened the lid. Then she wound it. It began playing, and I had to admit, it sounded real nice.

Tears came into Kate's eyes, and she sniffled a little.

"Don't you like it?"

"Like it? Ben, I love it. It's beautiful." She, too, gave me a hug. "What on earth made you do such a thing?"

"You mean buying the music box? I never gave it any thought. Guess it just seemed like something you'd want."

"It is, Ben. Are you hungry?"

"I'm starved."

"Then let's eat before supper gets cold."

Kate dug out a plate for me, we sat down at the table, and after she said grace, we dug in. Time we were finished eating, I didn't think I had enough room left to fit any of Kate's apple pie behind my belt. Only when she sliced a double portion and set it in front of me, somehow or another I found the space.

Feeling like a bull in a china shop, I helped Kate clear the table once we were done eating. Then, with a cup of coffee in my hand, I walked over to the door and looked out. The sun was sitting right above the horizon, and the sky was streaked with pink.

Kate came over and stood beside me. "Isn't it pretty tonight?" she said.

"Yes, ma'am, it surely is. You feel like taking a walk?"

"I'd like that very much."

We went to walking. It was hot, but not unpleasantly so, and we walked for some time, talking about everything and nothing. We finally started back when the sun was down for fear of stepping on a snake in the dark.

Back at the house, I sat down with another cup of coffee. Kate poured one for herself, and together we sat at the kitchen table. "How's the freighting business going?" Kate asked.

I shrugged. "Darby says we're going to need a couple of bigger wagons if we're to stand a chance of making the money we need."

"Can you get them?"

"Darby thinks we can find such, but doing it in time is the question. It looks like he'll be headed for Santa Fe come Saturday."

"So you won't be going out again for a time?"

I shook my head. "Soon as I can find a swamper. We need the money, Kate. If I can find a man, I plan on making another run come the first of the week."

"Oh. I was hoping you'd be around more. It seems we never see you. Todd's always asking where you are."

"I 'spect it's going to be this way for a year or two, even if we manage to get that land. After that, well, I've always wanted to get fat and lazy."

Kate smiled. "You may think you want it, Ben, but I suspect it'll never happen. You're a doer. You're always on the move, even when you're sitting still. You sit too long, and I can see you tightening up, just like an overwound clock. Pretty soon you're up on your feet, looking for something to do."

"Guess that's the trouble. Seems I've always been on the go. I never had no time to just sit and do nothing. There's always been work to do."

"Yes. Or places to go and things to see. I suspect you'll still be working when you're ninety, and probably still saying all you want to do is sit down in a rocking chair."

I had to laugh. "Might be you're right, Kate. But a man's got to have something to gripe about."

It was her turn to laugh. "I've never met a man who had to look very far to find something."

We talked a while, and at last I stood up. Todd had fallen asleep on the floor, and Laura was near there herself. "Guess I've kept you all up too late," I said. "Time I was headed back."

"I'm very happy you came," she said. "And not because of the music box. When will I . . . when will you stop and see us again?"

"I can't say for sure, Kate. Come Monday, I'll likely head out again. We can't let up much, or we'll never make it."

"What about Sunday dinner? There's no reason to miss that, is there?"

"Not that comes to mind."

"Good. I'll count on seeing you."

"Yes, ma'am. I'll sure be here."

Going out and climbing aboard Nugget, we trotted off into the night. After a bit, I looked back. Kate was still standing there in the doorway, looking my way.

It really wasn't much more than two skips and a long hop from Kate's place to ours, but that night it seemed worse than the trip to Santa Fe. When I finally did get back, I took the time to give Nugget a good rubdown. I let him drink, gave him a helping of grain, then went inside the house and struck a match.

I touched the match to the wick of a lamp, adjusted the flame. The house seemed emptier, quieter, and a damned sight unfriendlier than I recalled it being.

The fire in the cookstove was dead, but in no mood for sleeping yet, I rekindled it and put on a pot of coffee. Once the coffee was finished perking, I poured a cup and sat down at the table. I spent two hours drinking coffee and smoking those Cross Cut cigarettes.

Then I carried a cup of coffee onto the porch and spent another hour there.

There was no moon, and no clouds. The stars looked close enough to grab and bright enough to read by. That whole, long while I can't say I was really thinking about anything. Or maybe I was thinking about everything.

My mind ran back to the time when I was a kid, and long ago as that was, the feeling of it all came back to me. Sitting there with a cup of coffee in one hand, and a ready-made cigarette in the other, I wandered back to being a tyke.

I recalled going fishing with Jack Baily and Buddy Keith, and remembered clear how Wilma Denkins used to tease me on account of the cowlick I couldn't keep combed down. I remembered, too, the taste of a stolen kiss.

It had been Wilma I kissed, and though I thought about it for months afterward, I never could think of any good reason why I'd done it. We were always fussing and fighting, only one day we were talking about some homework the teacher had given us, and I kissed her.

I reckon I was more surprised than she was and likely turned as red. Her eyes opened wide, then she turned around and ran off without another word. I don't think either of us ever mentioned it again, but I don't recall us ever having another fight, neither.

I thought about going off to war, feeling we'd whip the Yankees and be home in time for Christmas. It hadn't worked out that away, and I sure came out of the war a different man than I'd been going in.

And I thought about Kate. And about Todd and Laura, and how that little house of Kate's seemed alive and warm and comfortable.

Finally I stood up, walked away from the porch a piece, and emptied my bladder. A coyote howled and received no answer. "I know how you feel," I said aloud. "I know just exactly how you feel."

Going back into the house, I carried the lamp into the bedroom. There I shucked my clothes, blew out the lamp, and went to bed. Sleep came, and with it dreams. It was a tossin', turnin', fitful sleep I had, and after no more than two hours, I gave up on it.

It felt like I'd had no sleep at all, but as long as I couldn't sleep proper, it seemed I might as well be busy. Thinking it would be near dawn by the time I reached Globe, I went ahead and saddled Nugget.

Unless a rain or such moved in, it might be up close to a hundred degrees before noon, but the night air was cool, almost cold. It woke me up, if nothing else.

When we reached Globe, it was still dark, though the first hint of dawn lay across the eastern horizon. A dog barked in the distance, was silent, then started barking again. A voice yelled, "Shut up, you mangy bastard." The dog shut up, at least for the moment.

I walked Nugget on down to the smithy, swung from the saddle. With Nugget's reins in my hand, I fumbled about in my pocket for the key to the padlock we'd put on the big front door. I found it, stretched it out for the lock.

Right at that moment something clanged inside the smithy. The clanging sound was followed immediately by the sound of a man's voice, just loud enough for me to hear.

"Goddamnit to hell!" the voice said.

Someone was inside the smithy. Darby? No, the deep growl I heard sure as anything didn't belong to Darby. Nor to Johnny or Billy. Who else might be in there?

Whoever it was, it didn't seem likely they were up to any good. No light at all showed from the inside, and the only reason anyone wouldn't have a lantern going was because they didn't want to risk being seen.

Dropping Nugget's reins, I eased my Colt from the holster, moved around the smithy. There were three other ways into the smithy: you could get in through the little room we'd converted to an office, through the sliding door at the back where we led horses in and out of the stalls, or through a small door on the east side that we seldom used. I moved around, checking each door.

The lock to the freight office had been pried loose. Easing the door open, I stepped inside.

Dawn was coming fast, but it was still pitch-black inside. By feel, I made my way across the freight office. When I stretched out my hand to find the door leading into the smithy, my fingers met only air. The door was already open.

I stepped through it and stopped. I couldn't see anything. It was so dark I could feel the blackness pressing in on my eyes.

Something moved. It was a scuffing sound I heard, the sound of boots easing across the floor, maybe. I could barely make out someone crouched fifteen feet away, turned sideways to me. Whoever it was held a lighted match cupped in his hands, just above a pile of straw. As I watched, he started lowering the match.

I thumbed back the hammer on the Colt, and the sound was loud in the stillness. The man's head snapped toward me. As bright as that match had seemed, it didn't really throw much light. But the man saw me, his eyes locking right onto mine.

"Mister," I said, "you snuff out that match and you won't live to see it hit."

For just a moment he hesitated, then suddenly shook his hand and the match went out. It was suddenly pitch black, seeming even darker than before. I couldn't tell where he was. Had he moved at all, or was he still huddled there on the floor?

Just as I heard him move, I felt the big shape charging toward me. There was no time to react. A shoulder struck my chest, driving me back through the doorway and into the office.

I was struck hard, but twisted enough so I took the fall on my shoulder rather than my back. The Colt flew from my hand, struck the floor, and exploded. In the flare from its powder flash, I got a brief glimpse of the man's face.

Then he was off me. The office door flew open, and he went through it at a run. I jumped to my feet, tripped over something, went down again. By the time I got up a second time and charged through the door, the man was gone. I'd no idea where he went, but he was sure enough gone.

It was only then that I felt the tingling in my little finger. Going back inside the office, I lit the lamp that Helen kept on her desk. By its light, I looked at my finger. The nail was gone, ripped off cleaner than a whistle. Once I saw the damage, the tingling sensation turned to pain.

Fact is, it hurt like a son of a bitch. "Hell's bells," I said. The pain increased, and so did my swearing. Wrapping the last clean bandanna I owned around the finger, I awkwardly tied it in place.

I picked up my Colt, then went into the smithy. I lit a lantern, then dug out a bottle of whiskey that we kept tucked away in the harness room. I took one long drink, then a second. While waiting for that to take effect, I took a third long drink, then poured a healthy dollop of whiskey onto the bandanna, letting it soak through to my finger. It stung like hell.

We had half a dozen big sacks of grain stacked against the wall right near the harness room, and I sat down on them to catch my wind. I leaned back against the wall to rest, and right there my lack of sleep and those three long drinks of whiskey caught up to me.

Be damned if I didn't fall sounder asleep than a bear in winter.

CHAPTER 17

IT WAS DARBY who woke me up by poking me with the toe of his boot. I'll tell you right now, opening your eyes and seeing a face like Darby's leaning over you ain't the best way in the world to wake up.

"You sleeping one off?" he asked.

My neck was stiff as a frozen snake. I leaned forward, rubbed my neck, took a drink of whiskey. "Wish that was the reason."

I ran through what had happened, and Darby swore.

"Did you recognize him?" Darby asked.

"No, I don't think I ever saw him before, but I'd sure know him if I ever run into him again."

"Murphy," he said. "That sounds like the kind of thing he'd send somebody to do."

"We hurting him that bad?"

"We ain't hurting him too much at all yet. I allow he's got thirty or forty wagons, all told. Hell, he's got hisself fourteen of those big bastard wagons that make ourn look small."

"So why would he waste his time worrying about us?"

"Well, you gotta remember he's put a whole lot of money into building up his freighting business. There was a time when the big wagons was called Murphy wagons. It wasn't on account of P. G. Murphy. Just a damn coincidence in names. Anyhow, folks started using wagons like that on account of the governor of Mexico.

"He went and slapped a tax on ever' wagon coming into Santa Fe, and that done it. It was a flat tax, meaning you paid the same no matter what size wagon you used, so

151

some of the freighters built a few wagons more'n twice the size of anything else that ever rolled freight.

"That was forty years ago, but those wagons worked out so well, folks kept using them. One of them damn wagons will hold three times or more what a Pittsburgh can haul. You've seen them out on the trails."

"Seen their dust, mostly. They sure raise a cloud when they run in caravans. But if we ain't hurting Murphy, why would he want to burn this place down?"

"I said we ain't hurting him much. But he's likely feeling a pinch. We got folks lined up for four, maybe five months. We're a sight cheaper than Murphy, and we'll haul freight right to a man's door.

"Besides, Murphy don't guarantee his loads like we do. He loses a load to the Apache, to outlaws, or to a twister, well, folks are out their money, though he does give back the freighting charges. So folks are willing to wait on us, when they don't need something right away. But if it be true that Murphy's strapped for cash money, he wouldn't like us taking loads away, no matter how few and small.

"And don't forget, Murphy—or somebody—sure put Richardson and the others out of business. It's my thought he just likes stepping on snakes before they're big enough to bite too deep."

"Well, if I find out Murphy was behind this, I'll sure go see him, and it won't be to talk."

"You going to tell the marshal about this?"

"I figured to mention it."

"What did the fella who done this look like?"

"Big and butt ugly is what I recall. Had a nose that looked like a squashed tomato."

"Be goddamn if that don't sound like Bull Harris. He's one of Murphy's bullwhackers. I ain't seen him about town for a time, though."

Standing up, I stretched out my back. "You reckon Doc Jefferies is up and about?"

"It's near eight. I can't see why anybody would sleep later than that. What'd you do to yerself now?"

I held up my left hand. "Ain't nothing. I lost a nail."

"Hell, you'd run to the doctor for that?"

"Figured I might, since I'm in town and all."

"Damned if you ain't gettin' soft, Hawkins."

"It hurts, goddamnit."

"That's what whiskey's for. Next thing you know, you'll be running to the sawbones when you cut yourself shaving."

"Well, kiss my arse, you old fart!"

Darby snorted. "Ain't no need to get testy. I'm just saying a body's got to watch how he pampers hisself, is all."

Shaking my head, I walked out, Darby trailing behind like an old hound dog. Doc Jefferies wasn't yet awake, as it turned out. Only his house was built right up against his office, and he heard me knocking. He yelled out to hang on a minute and he'd be there.

It took more like ten minutes, but at last he opened the door. His hair was all rumpled, his eyes still filled with sleep, but he let us in. "What seems to be the trouble?" he asked.

I slipped the bandanna off my finger and left him have a look. "You got me out of bed because of that?"

"Now you sound like Darby. I'll tell you the same thing I told him. It hurts, Doc."

"All right. Come on over here."

He led me to a washbasin, and once there he cleaned the wound and doused it with carbolic spray. Then he put a clean little bandage on it. Once he was done, he opened a drawer and came out with a peppermint stick. He handed it to me.

"I know it ain't much of a hurt," I said, "but you don't have to rub it in."

"It isn't that," he said. "Your breath smells like a distillery."

"I 'spect it does. I had to have something for the pain, didn't I."

"Just take a bite."

"I don't like peppermint."

"I don't care. Think of it as medicine."

"Ah, hell." I bit a hunk off the peppermint stick, chewed it up, swallowed. "You satisfied?"

"I will be when you give me a dollar."

I gave him a dollar.

Darby and me went on down to Molly's after that. Marshal Reynolds was just starting breakfast and we sat down with him. I went through what had happened, and Darby put in his part about the man sounding like Bull Harris.

"I'll look into it," Marshal Reynolds said. "Trouble is, even if it was Harris, I can almost guarantee he's out of Globe by now. Likely riding hell bent for some caravan of Murphy's.

"And you can bet every muleskinner on that caravan will swear Harris has been with them for two months. And even if they don't, it would still come down to your word against his. I wish you managed to hold him there at the smithy."

"If I come across the man," I said, "I'll hold my fist against his teeth."

Marshal Reynolds nodded. "Just don't kill him."

"I don't mean to kill him. Just plan to see if he can fight in the daylight, is all."

Me and Darby ate breakfast, and once we were done I lit up one of those Cross Cuts. Marshal Reynolds grinned. "You get started on those things, it's hard to go back to rolling your own."

"Never could roll them worth anything," I said. "Pa always said I had hands fit to hold a hammer and not much else. Guess he wasn't far wrong."

"You have big hands," Marshal Reynolds said. "Big and thick."

"Comes from hard work, I guess. Though my pa worked

his whole life long, mostly as a blacksmith, and he never had hands near the size of mine."

We sat and talked a time, and finally stood up to get to our doings. "You be careful, Hawkins," Marshal Reynolds said. "You know what they say about bad luck coming in threes."

"By God, Marshal. I wish you hadn't said that. Now I'll be looking over my shoulder."

"That's exactly what you should be doing. See you around."

I guess I did spend some time looking over my shoulder, but the next few days went along pretty well. On Friday morning, Billy came riding in. He'd changed enough from the time I met him only a year earlier that seeing him after the long freight run startled me. Pounding iron at the smithy had put hard muscle on his arms, shoulders, and chest.

In muleskinner fashion, he'd taken to cutting the sleeves from his shirt, and his arms and face were burned brown as mahogany. His hair was down on his shoulders, and he was sporting a thick mustache for the first time since I'd known him.

He wheeled those six mules and that big wagon around beside the smithy and hauled them to a stop like a man who'd been doing it since he was weaned from his mother's teat. And once they were stopped, he hopped down like a man with two good legs.

He grabbed my hand and gave me a big smile. "Goddamn, Ben, seems like I ain't seen you in ages."

"Feels like it. You have any trouble on your run?"

"Nah, lost a couple of mules, is all. How about you? Any trouble?"

"None to speak of."

We went down to O'Brien's, drank a couple of beers, and stuffed ourselves on ham sandwiches and pickled eggs. Then Billy went to clean himself up, planning to ride out and see Laura.

On Saturday, I gave Darby twelve hundred dollars and put him on the stage to Santa Fe, telling him to buy cheap and get back as soon as he could.

Sunday came, and me and Billy rode out to Kate's for dinner. We stayed until well after dark.

Monday, it was time to start making runs again. Going through the jobs that we had lined up, we saw a whole passel that would be quick and easy. Most of them were for freight Murphy had already brought in but hadn't carried all the way to where the folks wanted it.

Even in times when there wasn't all that much danger in being out on the trail, a lot of big freighters would only haul loads to the nearest town, and the customer would pick it up there in his own wagon. That was fine in places where the distance to the nearest town wasn't all that great, or the loads weren't too big to fit in a ranch or farm wagon. But Murphy was taking the practice to the limit.

Truth is, he just didn't want to pay what it took to get a man to drive a lone wagon through dangerous territory, and I suspected he didn't want to risk losing wagons and mules, either. Such things were costly as hell, and if it was true that Murphy was short on cash, he'd be cautious about the need to spend any. And being the only big freighter about, he could thumb his nose at folks who got a bee in their bonnet over having to haul the loads fifty or sixty miles on their own. 'Specially after they'd paid through the nose to have Murphy haul it part way.

In one sense, it was hard to blame Murphy. Freighting was a risky business, and he made ninety percent of his money hauling huge loads in those big wagons he ran in caravans. Loads like that were almost always for stores and such in towns, or for the larger copper mines. Those shipments he delivered right to the front door.

But it seemed to us we could make some quick money by hauling those short loads to folks at a reduced rate. Most of the loads were small, and intended for folks generally no more than thirty to fifty miles from Globe.

By stuffing our wagons to the brim, we figured we could get in seven or eight loads each and deliver them by swinging wide loops, me starting out southeast and swinging around to the west. Billy would start to the northeast and swing around to the northwest.

We figured the runs wouldn't take more than two weeks or so, unless we ran into trouble, and we'd make a tidy profit while gaining favor with new customers.

Trouble was, with Darby off to Santa Fe, we were going to be one swamper short. Although we called Darby a swamper, he was more a driver than I was, and he was teaching us all how to go about things. It was his knowledge that made him valuable, and we needed another man to take care of all the little tasks that needed doing, from cooking meals to caring for the mules, and other such. One man could drive and do all those other things, but he'd wear himself to a frazzle in the process.

But after hunting about town all morning for a swamper, I said to hell with it. I'd do my own damned swamping, and if I couldn't, then things would just have to go undone.

Every load we wanted was stacked under tarps down at Murphy's freight yard, and we went down there to pick them up. Those boys weren't none too happy to see us, and one of them ran to fetch Murphy. He came stomping along and asked what the hell we wanted.

I shoved our freight orders at him and said we were there to pick up our loads. He flipped through the pages, saw we really did have what we said.

"You're starting to annoy the hell out of me, Hawkins."

"Figured as much. Which reminds me, you can tell Bull Harris me an' him are going to go knuckle and skull next time I see him."

Murphy frowned. "Harris? Hell, he's not even in Globe. Or shouldn't be. What do you have against him?"

"Just want to teach him not to play with matches, is all. The son of a bitch tried to burn me out."

Murphy's face turned ugly. "I told you, he wasn't even around. And if you're trying to say I had anything to do with the trouble you've had, then maybe I ought to pull you down off that wagon and beat some sense into you."

"Anytime, Mr. Murphy. Just anytime at all."

For long seconds he met my eyes. "Find another line of work, Hawkins. This one doesn't suit you."

He turned around and walked off as hard-heeled as he came. And I wasn't fooled a bit. The only reason he hadn't tried yanking me down off the wagon was because it didn't suit his interests at the time.

We loaded up the freight, getting no help at all from any of Murphy's men. Not that I'd expected any or wanted any. Finally we were loaded right up to the rafters and set off on our way.

Once we were clear of Globe, I chunked a rock and caught the lead wheeler on the rump. Then I cracked that long bullwhip. "Get on there, you lop-eared sons o' bitches," I yelled. "We ain't got forever."

I was still waiting for the second leg of bad luck to drop, and I rode with my rifle right near my side a good part of the time. And I'd bought me a ten-gauge shotgun that was loaded with double-ought buckshot. It was a short-barreled Greener, and every time a jackrabbit hopped from the brush I grabbed for it. All my life I'd heard folks say a watched pot never boils, and I was hoping it followed that when you're on the lookout for trouble it never happens. In case I was wrong, I figured that big shotgun might dissuade it from doing me much harm.

CHAPTER 18

IT WAS THE first time I'd been out alone, and after a few days I allowed it would be the last time. It took three times as long to get things done. Between watering and grazing the mules, hitching them up and unhitching them again, I was losing time on the trail.

And that ain't even considering such things as building fires, cooking, and taking care of things that broke. I started running earlier each morning and stopping later at night, and it wasn't long before I was beginning to forget what sleep was.

The way that two-week run went, you'd have thought there wasn't an Apache or outlaw, or even a wheel-bustin' rock in the whole damned territory. I should've figured that was the lull before the storm.

Still, being out there on the trail was a fine thing most times. It was pleasant to sit about a fire again, listening to the night sounds drifting in from the darkness. And driving the team by day wasn't such a bad thing.

Thinking I might learn to read better, I'd brought along a couple of books. One of them was called *Moby Dick*, written by some fellow named Herman Melville. I tried to get started on it two or three times, but finally gave it up as a losing fight.

The other book was called *Twenty Thousand Leagues Under the Sea*. It was written by Jules Verne, and I'll tell you what, that book was something! I had to grab hold of a good many words and wrestle them down like an old mossybacked bull, but it was worth the doing.

Most of the story didn't seem real likely, I mean, folks

going about under the ocean, and even living there. But, by God, that story had me forgettin' all about what I was doing most times.

It was a wonder a bunch of Apaches or bandits didn't ride up and shoot me on the spot. Like as not, I wouldn't have seen them comin' till I was dead.

Not to say that trip went off perfect. One night three of the mules got loose, and it took me most of the next morning to track them down. Another time I let the mules get us over too near a washed-out spot along the trail. The wheels got into the loose sand there, and the whole damned side of the wagon slid down into the deep cut caused by the rain.

I got the mules stopped, but the wagon was tilting so far over I was afraid to let them try pulling it back out, for fear the whole thing would tip over.

There wasn't nothing else to do but unhitch the mules, then empty every damned piece of freight. Then I hitched the mules back up and managed to get the wagon out. Only by that time it was darker than the inside of bear's butt, so I had to stake out the mules as best I could, and make camp right there where we were.

Soon as it was light enough the next morning, I started reloading all that damned freight, and without Billy and his swamper there to help out, it turned into a four-hour job. Luckily, most of the freight was of a manageable size, but it was still a backbreaking, brutal job.

Then, while I was on the last leg of the trip, I saw the Apaches. Three of them, near invisible among some brush three hundred yards off the trail. They were riding along easy, watching me for certain.

Pulling the mules to a stop, I climbed into the cubbyhole and levered a round into my rifle. Those three Indians pulled up and sat there watching me for five minutes, yelling out things I could barely hear and couldn't understand at all.

Then one of them turned his horse around, yanked down the pants he was wearing, and wiggled his bare arse at me. They rode off a minute later, laughing like hell.

I dropped off the last load of freight and made it back to Globe a damned sight quicker than those mules wanted to go. I'd had all the trouble with Apaches I ever wanted, so I was relieved that all they wanted was to poke a little fun at my expense. I wished those three out yonder all the best, just so long as wishing that put plenty of distance between me and them.

Me and Billy figured to make our runs about the same length, and he came into Globe no more than five hours after I did, though we hadn't planned to cut it anywhere near that close. We rested a full day, then started right off on a good-sized run to one of the small copper mines. It was the first time we'd run wagons together, but it came off fine.

By the time we returned, Darby was back from Santa Fe, and with him he had two of the biggest damned wagons I'd ever seen. Bigger even than the wagons Murphy was running. Behind them he was towing a little bitty danged wagon that he called a repair caboose. "Each one of these big wagons'll hold five tons of freight," he said. "That ought to make us some good money."

I walked around the wagons. They were straight-sided affairs, really just giant boxes sitting on huge wheels and thick axles. There wasn't no sign of a seat that met my eye.

"Where'n hell does a man sit?"

Darby spat tobacco juice. "You walk along beside, if you got the mules trained and you ain't in much of a hurry.

"You want to go faster than a body can walk, the skinner straddles the left-wheeler . . . that's the mule closest to the left wheel.

"There's a pair of jerk lines running from the lead mules. You give one long pull to make them go left, and three or four little jerks to make them go right. They ain't much to it. Twixt that jerk line and a snapping whip, a body can get the job done."

"How many mules does it take to pull these bastards?"

"Twelve's the general rule. If you want more speed, or you figure there's a chance to lose a couple, you can go to fourteen or sixteen. Now and again I've known skinners who strung twenty mules out in front of these things.

"It all depends on what you're expectin' from the mules, what kind of a load you're hauling, and what kind of country you're haulin' it through. And skinners are the kind of bastards who sometimes get a notion to string up mules in ways that make no sense at all to anyone but them."

"They don't look to need much work," I said.

"No, sir. They're not far from new. Give 'em a coat of paint, grease up the axles proper, and they'll be ready to roll."

"How much did you have to pay?"

"Eight hundred for them and six old mules. Them mules wasn't worth nothing, and the freighter I got 'em from near gave 'em away. They was old and wore out, but I figured they'd do to get the wagons back here.

"I pushed them hard, and lost one. He just fell over and died on the spot."

"We got enough mules to keep all our wagons rolling?"

"Let's see, I figure sixteen to pull these wagons, eight each for the others, that's—"

"Thirty-two," I said.

"We won't be able to rest as many mules as I'd like," Darby said, "but I figure we got enough. Don't want to go losing too many, though.

"Might be we'll want to split these wagons up, and use two of the Pittsburghs as trailers. That way I'd not be afeared to run these wagons with fourteen mules, or even twelve, in a pickle."

"That'd give us two big loads we could send in different directions," I said. "Be some advantage in that, moneywise, at least. But we'll need another driver and a swamper. I tried finding a swamper, and couldn't get no takers."

"You didn't know whereabouts to look. Besides, we'll get by cheaper if I skin a wagon. That way we'll only need two swampers. Be a sight cheaper."

"Makes good sense to me."

Me, Billy, and Darby were all at the smithy near dark that same evening when Johnny rode in. He came with a grim look on his face. Alongside him was a hard-looking man I'd never seen before. Before he'd climbed from the saddle or said a word, I knew something was wrong.

He slipped off his horse, dropped to the ground, and looked at us. "We need to have a powwow," he said.

"What about?"

The second piece of bad luck came crashing down hard enough to make me think it must have been God throwing the rock.

"The horses we caught up," he said. "They got stole. It was that bastard Hoag Willis." He pointed to the fellow he rode into town with. "This here's Jim Reagan. He was one of them out there with me when it all happened. There were four of us."

"Let's go down to O'Brien's," I said. "We can hash it all out there."

We walked down to O'Brien's. Dunie saw the looks on our faces and knew right away something was wrong. He brought us beers and went back to the bar without saying a word.

Once we were sitting, Johnny took a long drink of beer, then rolled a smoke, lit it, and took another drink of beer. He looked tired, saddle weary. "It all worked out just like I figured it would," he said. "I built those fence sections, then hired four men from Phoenix to help me set them up.

"Those mustangs ran right into the trap slicker than grain through a goose. We got them fenced in, and that was that. We made a count and found sixty-three mustangs caught. Even after culling out those that were too old, or too broke down, we had thirty-nine head of the best horse-flesh you could want.

"That country is wild out there. Wild, empty, and pretty as anything. In all the while we spent there, we never saw another person. Not until it was too late.

"Since there were four of us, we decided to rough-break that string right there. Hell, we had plenty of food, water, tobacco, and privacy, so why the hell not? It sure seemed we could make the drive back to Phoenix easier if those mustangs knew who was boss.

"With four of us bouncing around on those mustangs, it didn't take long to get the job done. We knew most of them would need a little more work once we got back, but right till then, everything was going along as fine as you could want."

"When did Willis come into the picture?"

"On the drive back. Seemed like we'd no more than hit the main trail when it happened. They weren't looking for us . . . that I'd swear. It was just damn bad luck. We drove those mustangs right into 'em.

"Those boys cut loose without saying go to hell, or anything else. Joe Belcher went down in the first volley. He never had a chance. The rest of us started shooting back, and broke for the rocks. Me and Jim here made it. Carl Henkins didn't.

"I swear, Ben. Willis must have had fifteen men with him this time. They took that whole damn string of mustangs, and our saddle horses along with them. Took us three days to come across a place where we could get more."

I took a long drink of beer and lit a cigarette. Right then I felt lower than a snake's belly. We needed the money those mustangs would have brought in. If they were as good as Johnny said, and if they'd taken the time to rough-break them, we could figure on a hundred apiece, and maybe a few dollars more for the best ones.

"That's one hell of a tough break," Darby said.

"Goddamn Hoag Willis," Billy said. "Somebody needs to nail his hide to the barn door."

"There's no use crying about it now," I said. "We'll make up the money one way or another."

"To hell with the money," Johnny said. "He killed two men out there, and he stole our horses. I figure Billy's right. He needs his hide tacked up, and I know how to go about doing it."

"How's that?" I asked.

"We followed him," Reagan said. "Once we got hold of a couple of saddle horses, we followed him south. We crossed into Mexico and kept going. We followed him right to a little ranch down along the San Pedro River."

"We sure as hell did," Johnny said. "And we gave long thought to cutting those horses out and driving them back ourselves. But we couldn't think of a way to make it work with only the two of us."

"But you figure it would work with four of us?"

"It'd take four men, four good men, to pull it off. We have to drive those horses back across the border at night, and we'd have to push them like hell. Take at least four men to hold the bunch together."

"Do you think we could pull it off?"

"I sure mean to try. We rode by the fort on the way back, and I talked to Lieutenant Brice. He said those horse soldiers of his couldn't touch Willis unless they caught him on this side of the border, and the Mexican caballería didn't have no reason to bother him. Seems Willis is a good boy down across the border.

"I told Brice I could sure do something about Willis, and I didn't give a damn what country he was in. Brice said I'd be a fool to go after him down there, then he wished me luck just the same.

"I want those horses back, Ben. And if we can do it, I want Hoag Willis to pay for killing Joe Belcher and Carl Henkins—and for killing Todd's parents."

I thought a minute. "You sure we can pull it off? You dead sure?"

"Hell," Johnny said. "I ain't dead sure the sun'll come up in the morning. But I think we stand a good chance. Willis feels safe as a suckling child down there. You can tell by how he don't stand but one guard out, and lets that one sleep half the time.

"I'm telling you, Ben, he just doesn't figure anybody's going to bother him down there in Sonora."

"How long do you figure it would take? To get down there, drive out the horses, and get back here?"

"Ah, hell, let me think. What do you figure, Jim?"

He shrugged. "It's about a hundred and forty miles, or thereabouts. That's one way. If we push hard . . . ten days all told. Maybe less, but you have to figure we'll need a day or two down there just waiting for the right time."

Ten days was a long time to be gone. On the other hand, if we got those horses back, we'd make better than three thousand dollars for the time, and that was money we desperately needed.

While I was thinking, I glanced at Jim Reagan. He was looking at me, an expression on his face that matched my thoughts. I had a feeling I knew him from somewhere, but I couldn't place him. Someone from a long time back.

How far back? Twenty years, maybe? Was he old enough for that? Likely. I put him at forty or so. Then it came to me—my first drive up the Chisholm Trail to Abilene. I wasn't a hell of a lot more than a kid myself. It was right after the war, and I'd figured I'd seen all there was to see. Only Abilene was something altogether different. I'd never met an honest-to-God whore nor a professional gambler. Abilene had both in plenty. And both got a sizable share of my wages.

Abilene also had saloons that ran near the whole night through, cowboys, thieves, cattle by the hundreds of thousands, wild women, and wilder men.

It was a wild, boisterous, money-mad boomtown, and there was trouble a-plenty for the man who didn't watch his step. My second day there I'd seen a man killed. A big, tough-looking fellow with a tied down gun forced a fuzzy-faced kid into a gunfight.

I guess everybody watching figured that kid had seen his last day on earth. It didn't work out that way. The other fellow drew first, and he sure seemed fast to me. His Colt came out of the holster and that kid still hadn't moved. Then the kid drew and fired twice, so close together they sounded like one shot. I swear, if the two bullets through the chest hadn't killed the other fellow, the surprise might have.

Jim Reagan sure looked like an older version of that kid. Only the kid's name wasn't Reagan, it was James Tremain. Tremain eventually became a well-known gunfighter. It was said he'd killed twenty men, and that nobody on earth was faster with a Colt. Not Hardin, not Hickok, not anybody at all. As often as not, folks called him "Tenpenny"—he was said to practice shooting that Colt of his by drawing and firing at tenpenny nails. And he could drive those tenpenny nails into a tree from twenty yards, four shots out of five.

For ten years or so, his name had been spoken in saloons and around campfires in the same breath as the better-known gunfighters. Then he'd disappeared, and folks figured he'd either died or maybe gone back East.

Could this be him? It sure as hell looked like him. But yes or no, it was none of my business.

Going to the bar, I got a bottle of whiskey and five glasses. Carrying them back to the table, I poured drinks all around. "Most times I'd say let it lie. But we need that three thousand dollars, else we're going to lose that land. Might lose out on it anyway, but we'll sure as hell lose it without the money.

"We'll take a day to get things settled. Day after tomorrow, we'll ride down and see if Hoag Willis knows how to treat visitors who come calling by night. I figure the four of us ought to be enough."

"Four?" Darby said. "What about me? You ain't got the idea I'm gonna sit here and mildew, have you?"

"Nope. But I don't want the freight line shut down for ten days, neither. I figure you can take Poe as a swamper and do some hauling. Hell, with those big wagons you brought back, you can do more in one trip than we could've in three using the Pittsburghs."

"By God, it's a hell of a thing to leave a man out of a fight on account of money. That's all I got to say."

"If we do it right," I said, "there won't be no fighting to it."

We talked and drank for another hour, then I stood up. "Got an early day tomorrow," I said. "Guess I'll go crawl into the loft at the smithy and get some sleep."

"Not me," Johnny said. "I ain't so much as seen a woman in a month of Sundays."

Reagan stood up at the same time as me. "There enough room in that loft for two?"

"Plenty, so long as you don't mind spreading your blanket on hay."

"I've spread it on worse."

We walked down to the smithy and I lit a lantern.

"Seemed you were giving me the twice over back at the saloon," he said.

"Didn't mean no offense," I said. "You just reminded me of someone, is all."

"Mind if I ask who?"

Stopping in my tracks, I looked into his eyes. "A fellow I saw in Abilene once. His name was James Tremain. There was some called him Tenpenny."

When he spoke, his voice was low. "I haven't used that name in ten years."

"None of my business, one way or the other."

"You'll not tell anyone."

"Like I said, it's none of my affair."

"I'm obliged."

"I do have one question, though."

"What's that?"

"There any truth to the way you picked up the name Tenpenny?"

He grinned. "Some. I saw Hickok do it once . . . he hit three out of five, and as men will, I finally had to try it myself.

"I hit one nail solid, bent a second, and missed the other three clean. Though not by more than an inch or so. I never did hit more than three out of five, and that not very often. But you know how tales grow."

"Folks figured you were dead."

"Nowhere near it. Been ranching up in Montana for almost eight years. But this last winter near wiped me out."

"That what brung you to Arizona?"

"That's about it. I came to get a job that was promised. Only it turned out the fellow died. I met Johnny in Phoenix, and here I am."

"Catching wild mustangs is one thing. Riding down into Sonora is another. Seems like you're risking your life for mighty small pay."

We climbed up into the loft and stretched out our blankets. Reagan took off his boots, stretched out. "I guess Johnny felt it was my place to tell you, so I will. Joe Belcher was my wife's kid brother," he said. "When I get back home, I'll have to tell her he was killed."

He rolled over onto a propped elbow, looked at me.

"The least I can do is tell her the man responsible paid the price for it," he said.

"You go off half-cocked, and you could get us all killed."

"I'm not going to do anything foolish. I've got a wife and

three tall boys waiting for me back home. But if Hoag Willis should chance to walk into my sights, I won't pass up the shot, neither."

"That's fair enough. Best get some sleep. Morning comes early around here."

I blew out the lantern, eased down onto the straw. It felt like a feather bed to my tired old body. I closed my eyes, tried to think about something, but went to sleep before the thought was complete.

CHAPTER 19

NOW, I'VE ALWAYS been an early riser. Generally, the sun comes up and I'm there to greet it. And Jim Reagan was a rancher, so he was in the habit of getting up early himself. Point being, we both woke up with the sun.

We cleaned up a bit out at the trough, then walked down to Molly's for breakfast. We sat there waiting for our food, and about the time Molly brought it out, Billy and Johnny walked in. They joined us, and we started making our plans right then and there.

Johnny and Jim Reagan sketched a crude map for me and Billy that still had enough detail to let us know what we were getting into. They made it look easy, but I knew things had a way of turning bad without any notice at all. So I asked plenty of questions.

But I had to hand it to them. They had an answer for everything I asked.

We broke up after breakfast, each going about his own concerns. Johnny headed back down to O'Brien's, Billy rode out to see Laura, and I went down to the smithy to see how many of the backed-up orders I could take care of before daylight ran out.

I don't rightly know what Jim Reagan went off to do. He saddled his horse and rode out of town, saying he'd be back in a few hours.

Late that evening we got what might have been a break . . . or might have been the worst thing that could've happened. It was just too soon to say.

Lieutenant Brice came riding into town, stopped at the smithy. He told me about Johnny stopping by at the fort and said he'd been giving the matter some thought. What it was all leading up to was that he had an idea he wanted to talk to us about. He gave me a little of it, just enough to let me know the others needed to hear it.

Lieutenant Brice agreed to stick around town until all of us were back together. That turned out to be near dark. It was Billy who held things up. Get him out there with Laura Crenshaw, and I doubted a twenty-mule team could haul him back before he was ready.

Finally, though, we did get back together, and we sat down at O'Brien's with Lieutenant Brice to hear him out.

First thing he did was look around the table, meeting our gaze. Then he settled on Johnny. "Despite everything I told you, you're still planning to cross the border and try to get your horses back, aren't you?"

Johnny didn't hesitate. "Hell, yes. Willis has been raiding this territory too damned long. He's raped, murdered, and stole folks blind. If those soldiers of yours can't stop him, we can at least let him know some folks won't take it sitting down."

"Besides," I said. "We need those horses back, else we're going to lose out on a deal we've staked a whole lot on."

"I'd still like to talk you out of making the attempt," he said. "Is there any chance at all that I can do it?"

We looked at each other. "No," Johnny said. "We're going after those horses."

"And if I get the chance," Reagan added, "I'm going after Hoag Willis himself." He laid out how Joe Belcher had been his wife's kid brother.

Lieutenant Brice took a sip of beer, pulled out a pipe, tamped it full of tobacco, lit it. Then he looked around the table again.

"Hoag Willis has had so much success because he keeps track of where our patrols are. He never hits anyplace where we stand a chance of catching him before he crosses the border.

"He knows we can't follow him across, and he never breaks the law down there, meaning the Mexican forces have no reason to bother him.

"It's a long, long border between Mexico and Arizona, and Willis never crosses the same place twice. If we knew where he was crossing and when, we could put an end to his raids once and for all. That's where you come in."

"Go ahead," I said. "You told me enough to make my spine crawl. May as well do the same for them."

"All right. My guess is, you intend to get those horses out as quietly as possible, right? If you can, you'll get up close to whoever's guarding the horses, bend a gun barrel over their head, and ease the horses out. Then, when you're far enough away so Willis and his men can't hear you, you'll start the horses running like hell and hope to cross the border before he knows what happened?"

"That's about the size of it," Johnny said. "Don't know if it'll work out quite like we want."

"I plan on going back after the others are clear away with the horses. I'll make a little noise and cut Willis from the herd while everything is all confused," Reagan said.

"There might be another way," Lieutenant Brice said. "Suppose you made enough noise to get Willis's attention right away. How far do you think he'd chase you?"

"Till hell and gone," I said. "He's not going to like anybody sneaking into his back yard."

"No, sir, he won't. Those horses are stolen property, but Hoag Willis has them, and he believes they're his. The question is, can you stay ahead of him until you reach the border?"

"If we get a ten-minute head start, we might. But Willis won't stop at the border, and once daylight comes, he'll catch us sure."

Lieutenant Brice took out a map, unfolded it, and asked where Willis's ranch was. Johnny pointed at the spot. "That's good," Brice said. "That's just about perfect. The

best way to keep that herd together at night will be to keep
the river at your side while you're running them. Do you
think you can time it so you can run them over the border
right along the river, and just a little after dawn?"

"We can," I said, "but we'd planned to start the ball rolling a lot earlier. We wanted to have the border a lot of miles
behind us by the time dawn came around. Considering
what you have in mind, I guess we can wait till later in
the night."

"Just exactly what do you have in mind?" Billy asked.
"And how many of us is it gonna get killed?"

"None, I hope," Lieutenant Brice said. "But what I have
in mind is this. "We can't cross the border after Willis, and
we never know when or where he's going to cross back over
and strike. This time, if you cooperate, we may be able to
change that.

"Willis usually crosses the border with no more than ten
to fifteen men, but we think he has as many as thirty-five.
If he has, they may all be on your tail.

"Now, officially, we can't send anyone across the border
to lure Willis back over. But since you're going anyway, if
you cross the border when and where I say, I'll have
enough soldiers lying in wait to give Willis and his men a
real surprise."

We spent a good minute looking back and forth at each
other. Billy finally broke the silence. "We get back across
the border, I 'spect things'll work out fine. Only, what if
Willis and his men catch up with us before we get back to
the border?"

"You planned on running those horses back by night,
didn't you? I'll be damned if I know how you expect to
cross some of that country by night at a full gallop, but you
must know your business."

"We've all been drovers," I said. "Running those horses'll
be child's play next to fighting a stampede by night.

"You want something to make you pray, just try keeping

up with three thousand head of stampeding beeves during a thunderstorm when the night's so black you ain't even sure your eyes are open. The only time you can see a damned thing is when lightning tears across the sky. And when it does, you see those big, longhorned beeves all around you, and maybe a gully or something so close you wonder how your horse missed running into it.

"No, sir. Running those horses back by night ain't going to be no easy doings, 'specially not with Willis and his men hot on our trail, but I'll take it over a cattle stampede any day of the week."

"Amen to that," Reagan said. "Driving those horses back will be like a Sunday ride with your girl compared to a cattle stampede by night."

"If you say so," Lieutenant Brice said. "I'll stick to the cavalry. All I have to worry about is getting shot, and putting up with fools from Washington. Of the two, I'd have to think hard about which is worse."

We sat there a time hashing out the what, where, and when, then Lieutenant Brice shoved back his chair and stood up. "I have to be leaving," he said. "But if everything goes right, I'll see you all again on the twenty-third. Bright and early."

"Don't be late," I said. "Else we're going to be four very unhappy men."

Lieutenant Brice grinned, walked out, lifting a hand in farewell. We watched him go, then Billy shook his head.

"What if he *is* late," Billy said. "That'll likely be the last morning we ever see."

"I 'spect he'll be early," I said. "He wants Willis more than any of us."

"Not more than me," Reagan said. "Not more than me."

There was no need to leave early the next morning, but we didn't figure to lie in bed all day, either. So once we finished the beer in front of us, we called it a night.

Johnny being Johnny, he waited till the first of O'Brien's

gals went by the table, grabbed her about the waist, and headed for the stairs. There was no doubt about where he'd be spending the night.

The rest of us walked over to the smithy and crawled up into the hayloft. We opened the loft door to let some air in, then stretched out on our blankets. I went to sleep wondering how in hell a man could start with no more of a dream than wanting to open a smithy, and end up riding into Mexico on a damn-fool trip to steal horses from a man who'd as soon kill us as eat his breakfast.

I finally concluded it came about 'cause I was heavy on muscle and light on brains. There wasn't nobody about who'd argue the point with me, so I went on to sleep.

We awoke early and got down from the loft before the sun could heat it up too much. We ate breakfast, bought enough supplies to get us through a ten-day trip, cramming it all into burlap sacks we could throw across our saddles.

By that time, Helen was in the freight office, Darby sitting right alongside her. We took a few minutes to go through the freight Darby ought to haul while we were gone, and then the four of us rode out.

We went by Kate's so Billy could say goodbye to Laura, and I guess it was in me to see Kate, as well. I'd no idea how well Billy's courting of Laura was going. Figuring it was none of my business, I hadn't asked. But as we were making ready to leave, I'll be damned if Laura didn't throw her arms around Billy's neck and kiss him full on the mouth. Seemed to me Billy was more surprised than any of us.

Laura finally let him go, and blushing red and pretty as any rose, she turned around and darted into the house. Then Kate walked up close to my horse and looked up at me. "You come back, Ben," she said. "Don't you dare get yourself killed."

"I'll come back, Kate. You can count on it."

"That's exactly what I'm doing."

Right then, looking down into Kate's eyes, the last thing on earth I wanted to do was go riding off anywheres.

So with Kate standing there looking like the family pet had just died, and with Laura and Todd both sad-eyed, we pointed our horses south and rode off to show everyone exactly how foolish men can be.

Turned out I wasn't the only one with those feelings running through me. After a mile or so, Billy cut his horse over close to mine. "Ben, you recollect saying one time that the dumbest critters on a trail drive weren't the cows nor the horses, but the drovers pushing them?"

"Yes, sir," I said. "Don't know as those were my exact words, but they're close enough."

"You were right, Ben. You were right as rain in spring."

CHAPTER 20

SOUTH WE RODE, trying to stay away from beaten trails and hoping to see nobody. We didn't, at least till we wished.

Not wanting to risk any of Willis's men seeing us when we crossed the border, we rode west, coming through Nogales and replenishing a few supplies while there. We left Nogales still heading south, figuring to come up on Willis's place from behind.

By God, that was wild, hot, desolate country! I'd not thought it could get much hotter than it'd been up in Globe, but it did. It got hotter than the sunny side of hell.

We rode slow, trying to save the horses for what lay ahead, but even at that, they dragged along with their heads low. We took to climbing down and leading them for long spells, and that seemed to help them, though it didn't do much for us.

Since he'd spent the last eight years up in Montana, I'd thought Jim Reagan would be taking the heat the hardest, though I didn't figure it would get the better of him. He was too tough a man to let near anything do that.

Still I kept my eye on him, right up till he caught me.

"No need to worry about me," he said. "I grew up in Kentucky, but I spent a few years in Texas. I know how the heat can get to a man."

"I always favored the heat," I said. "Never could understand how a body could live in a place cold enough to freeze his spit before it hit the ground."

"Winters up there can be a damned inconvenience," he said. "A bad one can kill a man's cattle so quick there's nothing to be done about it. But I like it. There's something fine about the way a good fire feels when it's thirty-below outside.

"I've had cabin fever a time or two, and sometimes me and my wife would get to snapping at each other after being snowed in for a month, but for the most part, it's a fine thing.

"And right now, I'd give a lot for a decent snowstorm. Or even a cool breeze."

"Can't argue with that."

We rode on, finally getting up close to where we wanted to be. Johnny and Jim had both been there before, and they gave us the tour. Camping well away, we waited till just before dawn to go ahead and take our look.

Stretched out on a ridge a quarter mile away, we waited for the sun to come up. When it did, I saw the prettiest little hacienda you can imagine. The main house was built of adobe, and had a tiled roof. It was big, spread out, and you'd sure not have thought a man like Hoag Willis would live there.

The horses we wanted were grazing in a big fence-enclosed pasture that started two hundred yards or so from the house. Close, maybe too close. And there were more horses than he'd stolen from us. I counted sixty-three, all told.

It appeared most of Willis's raiders lived right there with him. A pair of long, low bunkhouses squatted forty or fifty yards from the house, and a big corral held enough horses for fifty men.

While we watched, roosters started crowing and the men inside the bunkhouses woke up.

They started filing out, heading for one or another of four outhouses that sat some distance beyond, or walking straight to another building that we figured to be a kitchen. We counted forty-two men.

"By God, there's a bunch of them, ain't they?" Billy said.

Jim Reagan smiled. "Enough to go around."

"I'd bet we ain't seeing them all," I said. "Looks like Lieutenant Brice was wrong on his count."

"Thirty-five, or twice that number," Johnny said, "if they catch us we're in a boatload of trouble."

"That's not what I was thinking," I said. "I was just hoping Lieutenant Brice brings along enough soldiers. If he's thinking Willis will have thirty-five men charging along behind us, and it turns out there's fifty or more, it could make a difference."

"It could, at that," Jim said. "We'll just have to hope he knows his business. It's been my experience that a good officer will always figure the enemy has twice as many men as the reports say."

"I hope to God Brice is a good officer," Billy said, "else this surprise could run the other way."

"Nothing we can do about it now," I said. "Best we back on out of here before somebody spots us."

We scooted back off that high country, and rode to where we'd set up camp. We were better than four miles from the hacienda, and figured there wasn't much chance of anybody coming across us by accident.

We spent two days there, waiting so we could cross over the border when Lieutenant Brice and his men were supposed to be waiting. The day of the twenty-second came in hot, and the night didn't cool things down much.

We tried to sleep, though we took turns standing guard all night. We'd been paying attention to the time the sun came up, going by Jim Reagan's pocket watch, and three hours before dawn we all had breakfast behind our belts.

Finally Johnny kicked sand over the fire. "Best get to it," he said. "We wouldn't want to keep Lieutenant Brice waiting."

We saddled up and rode to that high spot again. There was just enough moonlight to let us see those horses, and the nighthawk riding guard. He was riding around the outside of the big pasture, and for a few minutes we debated what to do about him.

"Hell," Johnny said, "let's just ride up to him casual like. We'll be right on top of him before he knows we ain't some of his friends."

Lacking a better idea, that's how we handled it. We rode up at a trot, and by the time that fellow realized something was wrong, he had four guns sticking in his face. You never saw a man so ready to please.

We tied him to a fence post, gagged him with a bandanna, moved down a piece, and began cutting fence. It didn't take but five minutes to cut a big gap. Riding slowly into the pasture, we eased the horses into a group then through the gap in the fence.

We'd figured to make some noise to be sure those boys were on our tail when we crossed the border, but I'd no intention of getting anybody killed in the process. I let the other three push the horses slow for a time while I stayed behind.

Once I figured they had a good head start, I eased my rifle from the scabbard, levered a round into the chamber. I started to fire my rifle into the air, but thinking to make Willis double mad, I changed my mind and leveled the rifle at the house.

I couldn't see the sights very well by moonlight, but a house is a big target. Aiming right at the center, I squeezed off a round. The rifle sounded like thunder in the still of the night. I fired twice more, not knowing where the bullets were striking.

Then men started pouring from those bunkhouses, and somebody inside the house lit a lamp. That lamp put enough light inside the house for me to aim by, and I squeezed off three quick rounds. The sound of breaking glass came to my ears, and the lamp went out.

Figuring I'd raised enough hell, I slipped the rifle back

into the scabbard, stuck Nugget with both spurs. He took off like a jackrabbit, and I let him have his head.

Well up ahead, I could hear the pounding hooves of the horses we'd stolen, and in what seemed an awful short time, I started hearing the same sounds from back yonder. It had taken Willis and his men no time at all to get their own horses saddled and on the move.

There was enough moonlight to see anything of a good size, but not enough to let me pick out any details. All I could do was trust Nugget to see what was in his path, and hope to God he didn't step in no kind of hole.

Nor was there any way of saying how much time had passed. It seemed like hours were going by, but I knew it couldn't have been more'n twenty minutes or so. How far to the border? How long till dawn? Was I gaining ground on Johnny and the others? How far back were Willis and his men?

I just didn't know. Nugget was still running in stride, and I tried to close off my mind and not think about anything except hanging on.

Minutes passed, though I couldn't tell how many. A few shots rang out behind me, but where the bullets went, I had no idea. Twice Nugget stumbled, near throwing me the second time. Each time he recovered and we drove on, me not knowing who was gaining on who.

Then, almost as sudden as if God had struck a match to his own lamp, it was dawn. One minute I couldn't see a thing, and the next I could see too damned much.

There, no more than a hundred yards in front of me, I could see the string of horses we'd stolen. Then shots rang out, again, and this time a couple of the bullets came close enough for me to see the dust they kicked up. Glancing back over my shoulder, I saw what looked like an army charging to beat the band, and they all had me in mind.

Nugget was starting to labor, and I wondered where in hell the border was. Over in Texas, a man knew he'd crossed the border when he splashed across the Rio Grande, but here it wasn't so easy to tell.

Fact is, most places there wasn't no way at all of telling, though here and there you'd come across a sign.

But it sure as hell seemed like we'd ridden far enough to be back in our own damned country. Where'n hell was Lieutenant Brice and his men? If they didn't show up on time, there wouldn't be any of us left to complain.

Not having to worry about keeping other horses going where I wanted, I'd been making up some ground on Johnny and the others . . . and so had all those men back yonder. I'd closed the distance to no more than twenty-five yards, and Willis and his men were close enough to start shooting with some accuracy.

A bullet sang past my ear like an angry bee, and a horse went down up in front of me. Then several more shots rang out, and Nugget shuddered. I had just enough time to kick loose from the stirrups before he fell, sending me head over teakettle.

I hit hard enough to rattle my teeth, but started scrambling for cover before I'd stopped tumbling. The area didn't have much to hide behind, but I crawled behind the nearest rock and drew my Colt.

Those men were bearing right down on me, no more than fifty yards away. I thumbed back the hammer, knowing it wasn't going to do no good at all. Then a horse slid to a stop beside me and Jim Reagan was there. He stuck out his arm and I grabbed it, swung up behind him.

A hail of shots rang out, and I figured every manjack back there had fired at once. I braced myself for a bullet in the back. It never came. Then I heard the sounds of horses screaming and men yelling, all mixed in with the damndest bunch of volleyed rifle fire I'd heard since the war.

Looking back over my shoulder, I saw the carnage. The

land about didn't look fit to hide a jackrabbit, but of a sudden it had blossomed blue soldiers. They rose up all over hell and gone, and when they fired it tore Willis and his men to doll rags.

Then I saw the cavalry charging in from two sides, and just like that, it was over.

Reagan hauled his horse to a stop, and we went walking back. Johnny and Billy were backing the herd down.

Willis and forty-eight of his men had been on our trail. Of that number, seventeen were dead, and another twelve were wounded. The rest saw what they were up against and put up no fight. They looked plumb shocked at what had happened.

Willis himself had been cut to ribbons. He'd been right out in front, and it seemed like half the soldiers had lined their sights up on him.

Lieutenant Brice led his horse over to where we stood. His face was grim. "I never much cared for killing men," he said, "but in this case it doesn't seem to bother me."

"No reason it should," I said. "They sure didn't care when they were the ones doing the killing.

"Well, I'm glad it's over."

"You had me some worried. I was beginning to think you weren't going to show, or else that we'd got our days mixed up."

"We couldn't come in too early," he said. "The last thing we wanted was somebody riding down and telling Willis we had troops heading this way.

"We rode all night and had just got the men deployed when we saw your dust. You all right?"

"Guess we are. I sure lost a good horse, though."

"I've had it happen. Sometimes it's like losing a friend."

"Yes, sir, it sure is."

While Lieutenant Brice and his men tidied things up, Billy cut me a horse from the mustangs, and I threw my saddle over it. It was a big bay, and a fine horse, but it wasn't Nugget. It went to bucking when I threw my leg over, but I stayed with it until it decided I was boss.

We didn't make out as well with the horses as we'd hoped. What with lost strays in the night, we had forty-seven still together, but half those had been branded. There were four separate brands, and all were likely stolen.

Those we couldn't sell at all. We cut them loose, leaving us just twenty-three head. That would still give us two thousand dollars or so, but it wasn't going to be enough. Unless a miracle happened we were going to come up short.

We drove the horses back to Phoenix, thinking that to be the better market. A fellow offered us eighteen hundred for the lot, and while that was a little low, we took it. We sure couldn't take the time to sell them off one by one, and eighteen hundred was fair enough. But I knew we were going to come up short.

We headed back to Globe, at least me, Johnny, and Billy did. Jim Reagan figured it was time to head north again. Rightfully speaking, Johnny had hired him on at a dollar a day, but I gave him two hundred extra, though he complained he didn't have it coming.

After some argument, he took the money, and we shook hands. "You take care of yourself," he said.

I grinned. "You too, Tenpenny."

He returned the smile and trotted his horse off to the north.

CHAPTER 21

ONCE WE WERE settled in back in Globe, we all got with Helen and went to tallying up our money. Even with that eighteen hundred for the horses, and counting the one or two freight runs we might still make, we were going to come up short. Somewhere around three thousand dollars short, if Helen's numbers were right.

We'd figured to have the ten thousand near right on the money, and if we'd hired Helen soon enough, or got ourselves those big wagons early enough, we might have made it, though it still would've been close.

The main trouble was that none of us really knew all that much about running any kind of business. We could run cattle, or operate a smithy, but the ledger side of it all was something we'd no experience with.

There at the smithy, we just hadn't worried about it none. If we made enough to meet our bills and still have a few dollars in our pockets, we just didn't care about much else.

The freighting business was different. We'd had to pay other folks' wages, we'd had more expenses than a body could shake a stick at, and we simply hadn't taken it all into account.

Still, we went ahead and did all the freight hauling we had time for, counted our money, and went down to the bank to face the music.

Mr. Wilcox seemed happy enough to see us, right up until we told him we'd come up short on our count.

"How much do you have?" he asked.

"Seven thousand, three hundred and eighty-four dollars," I said. "That's counting it down to the change in our pockets."

Mr. Wilcox got up, walked to the window and stood there looking out a time, his hands clasped behind his back. Finally he came over and sat down again.

"To be honest," he said, "I really didn't think you would come this close . . . I'm probably a damn fool for suggesting it, but there's still a way you might own the land you want."

"How's that?"

"I suppose the bank could advance you the three thousand you need against your freighting business. In fact, from what you've told me, I think we could go to five thousand. That would give you a couple of thousand dollars in operating capital. But you should understand how unlikely it is that you'll be able to repay everything on time.

"In essence, you'll be paying the bank on three separate loans, and the payments on the land and on the freighting business will be quite high."

"Mr. Wilcox," Billy said, "I'm beginning to wonder if you ain't the devil himself."

"Other people have said as much," he said. "And I can sometimes see their point.

"But I won't lie to you about anything. I told you before that I doubted you would succeed. I doubt it twice as much if you accept this offer.

"Especially since this territory is suddenly appearing much safer. You helped eliminate Hoag Willis and his men, and now it appears Geronimo will soon be surrendering to the army."

"I hadn't heard," I said. "What's that got to do with us?"

"With this territory suddenly seeming safer, more people than ever will be moving here . . . and so will more freighting outfits. Even P. G. Murphy won't be able to keep them out.

"You and Murphy will both have to cut your rates. That will mean lower profits and a tougher time paying back the bank."

"There'll likely be Indians and outlaws and other folks stirring up trouble in this territory for years to come," I said. "Hoag Willis and Geronimo weren't the only troubles."

"No," Mr. Wilcox said, "they certainly were not. But the country will seem safer, and that is what will affect freighters moving in.

"Still, if you can make that land out there turn a profit within two or three years, you may stand a chance of success. At least, I'm willing to bet the bank's money that you will. But it's up to you."

"Can we have a day to think it over?"

"Certainly."

We thought it over, and argued it up one side and down the other. In the end, we figured it was as well to be hanged for a goat as a lamb. We accepted Mr. Wilcox's loan, in other words. And just like that, we were so damned far in debt that I didn't even know how many zeros to tack on after the first number.

Luckily, Helen did know. Seemed to me she was the only one of us that business couldn't do without.

Darby sure thought so. Be damned if he didn't ask her to marry up with him. And be double-damned if she didn't say yes.

Billy asked Laura the same question, but his answer wasn't quite the one he wanted. Laura said she loved him, but she was going East. Some relative yonder had said Laura could stay there while going to some fancy school or another. She would be gone two years and asked Billy would he wait for her. He said he would quick enough, but he went to moping around like a lost puppy.

Then it happened. We'd been waiting for the third piece

of hard luck, and in truth, I'd been hoping Laura heading back East was it. Either it wasn't, or our bad luck was running in fours.

We got us the biggest freight order we'd yet had, and set about getting it hauled. We had to go all the way to Santa Fe to pick it up, and it took both those big wagons, plus two of the Pittsburghs.

Darby and Johnny were leading the way back in those damned big wagons, while me and Douglas Poe were bringing up the rear with the Pittsburghs. Along about seven in the morning, not too long after we'd gotten underway, be damned if a rattler didn't start slithering across the road in front of us.

Instead of taking off, it coiled up and bit one of the mules. All hell broke loose. That mule went to kicking and trying like hell to break itself loose from the team. Me and Joe waded in and got things under control, but I doubted there was much hope at all for the mule.

I told Darby and Johnny to go on ahead, and we'd catch up once I had that mule cut loose and the team straightened out proper. They went on hauling, and me and Douglas went to work.

It was hotter'n hell, and those mules were all skittish as a chicken in a fox den after that rattler. I did what I could for the bit mule, then tied it along behind the wagon until we saw whether or not it was going to make it. It took us an hour to get moving again.

Then we came to the crest of a long, low hill, and there sat Darby's wagons not more than four hundred yards away. Only Darby and Johnny were on the ground, some fellow facing them with a gun. Two or three other men were in the wagons, heaving the freight out over the side. I couldn't quite be sure, but it looked like the men were wearing hoods, or some such.

We couldn't afford to lose that freight. We'd have to pay for it, and we didn't have nowhere near the cash. Any other time we might've, but right then most of our money had gone to get hold of the land.

Those folks gave no sign of having seen us, so I wheeled our wagons over into the brush, grabbed the big shotgun, and took off. I ran through the brush and finally came to a spot where I was no more than twenty yards from those wagons.

Darby and Johnny saw me at about the same time, but the fellow holding a gun on them had his back to me.

I thumbed back the hammers on the shotgun and stepped right out into the open. "You'd best drop that Colt," I said.

Instead of doing like he was told, the man spun around, trying to bring the Colt into line. Holding low, I pulled a trigger on the shotgun. It boomed like a cannon and swept the man's feet out from under him. Those boys up there in the wagon popped their heads up to see what had happened. The sight of that shotgun seemed to make them real gentle.

Johnny had grabbed the fallen man's Colt, and between us, those fellows must not have liked the odds. They came down from the wagons meek as lambs. Right then I had them yank off those flour-sack hoods.

One of the men was Bull Harris—the same bastard who had tried to burn us out. "By God," I said. "I was wondering when we'd meet again."

"I don't know what you're talkin' about," he said.

"The hell you don't! I've been wondering if you were as tough by day as you are in the dark."

"If you didn't have that shotgun, I'd be glad show you."

I tossed the shotgun to Darby and swung from the hip all in the same move. My fist caught Harris in the nose and I felt the bone give way. He staggered back against the wagon, caught his balance, wiped blood away from his face with the sleeve of his shirt.

Then he raised his fists and started toward me. He was

three inches taller and thirty pounds heavier than me, but at least part of that weight was in his gut. And he was no kind of fighter.

Like as not, he made his way through life on size and strength, bullying those who were smaller and weaker. But he had no idea how to handle his fists.

He swung a wild, looping right, and I went under it, then slammed him three times in the pit of the stomach. Every bit of the wind left him, and his face went white. He tried to fall to his knees, but I grabbed a handful of shirt and straightened him up.

Swinging with everything I had, I caught him right on the side of his chin. He folded up and went down like an old dishrag.

"Damn," Johnny said. "That wasn't hardly worth the trouble."

I was still mad. "Darby, you reckon you can handle both teams without me for a few days to a week?"

"Hell, yes. Long as we stay close together, the three of us can do 'er."

"Good. I'm going to round up these boys' horses and head back to Globe."

Johnny grinned. "You got in mind what I think?"

"I 'spect so."

"From all I hear, P. G. Murphy is a sight tougher than this fellow was."

"I hope so. Wouldn't be worth the ride, otherwise."

"By God," Darby said. "I'd like to be there."

"I'll tell you all about it. Or Murphy will."

We bandaged up the one fellow's feet . . . He'd taken five buckshot all told, and wouldn't be walking right for a time, but none of the buckshot had hit anything serious, and he'd live.

Those fellows had four horses, but I doubled them up on two just so they wouldn't think of bolting off. I rode a third horse, and turned the fourth loose after stripping it of gear. Then we pushed for Globe, with me prodding them all the way.

We came into town not long after noon, and I headed those boys straight to Marshal Reynolds. I told him my story. "If they won't talk," he said, "there's nothing I can do about Murphy."

"I'll handle Murphy."

"If you shoot him, I'll have to arrest you."

"Don't mean to shoot him. Folks say he's tougher than any muleskinner in the territory. Guess I'm going to find out."

"Fist fighting is against the local ordinance," Marshal Reynolds said. "I'll have to come along and break it up. You can expect me right after I have a late lunch."

"Marshal, if this fight isn't finished before then, I'll be hoping you do break it up."

Leaving the jail, I walked straight down to Murphy's freight yard. A bunch of men were milling around, pretending to work, and I told one of them to get Murphy.

"What do you want him for?"

"I mean to tear down his meathouse."

"What! Why, you damned fool, they ain't nobody ever whupped him with their fists. Way I hear it, he used to fight in the prize ring back East."

"I still mean to try."

The man looked me up and down. "You got the build for fighting," he said. "It might be worth watching at that. Only Murphy ain't here. He's down to Molly's getting his lunch."

Without saying another word, I turned and started walking. Near every man in the freight yard followed me. Seems they told everyone they passed as well, 'cause by the time we reached Molly's, there must have been forty, fifty folks trailing behind me.

Going into Molly's, I saw Murphy sitting at a corner table, sipping coffee. "Bull Harris tried to destroy a load of my freight," I said.

He wiped his mouth with a napkin. "What does that have to do with me?"

"I figure you put him up to it."

"What if I did?"

"You ain't denying it?"

"I'm not saying yes or no. And in case you're thinking about using that Colt, I'm not armed."

I unbuckled my gunbelt and dropped it onto a table. "I mean to whup you."

Murphy laughed. "By God, I always knew you were a fool."

"Just you get up and come outside."

I walked on out, and thirty seconds later, Murphy followed. From the corner of my eye, I saw Marshal Reynolds standing in the crowd.

Murphy stripped off his jacket, rolled up his sleeves. His arms were corded knots of muscle. He walked up to me, smiled. Then he hit me with no warning at all. His fist caught me on the cheek and next thing I know I was sitting on my arse, feeling like I'd been kicked by a mule.

I could feel my cheek swelling, and my head rang like an anvil. I spat, looked up.

"You won't whip me sitting there," Murphy said. "Stand up and let's get this over with."

Wondering what I'd gotten myself into, I stood up. We went toe to toe then, and for a time he was getting the better of it. Then I caught him in the short rib with a left and followed with a right that split his lip wide open. He staggered back, right into the left I brought up from Mexico, and he went down.

He dabbed at his lip. "Seems you can fight," he said. "Now we'll see just how well."

He stood up, and we went at it again. He knocked me

down twice, and would have a third time if I hadn't staggered against a hitching post. My chest was heaving, my breath coming in ragged gasps, and one eye was swelled near shut.

But I'd been getting my own licks in, and Murphy's face was as bloody and swollen as mine felt. He charged in, and I swung with a strength I didn't know I had left. I caught him hard right under the breastbone, feeling the shock up to my elbow.

He gasped, dropped to his knees. Only I'd already swung a left. It went over his head, and the swing of it took me to the ground. I was that weak.

I came to my knees just in time for Murphy to land a fist right on the side of my neck. It knocked me over. Somehow, I got back to my feet. My shirt was torn, my pants bloody. Murphy's fine shirt was ripped open so I could see the bruises forming on his stomach and ribs.

He climbed to his feet, and after looking at each other a few seconds, we went toe to toe again. Murphy hit me twice, but I already hurt so bad I didn't even feel those two punches. I hit him in the teeth, caught him on the temple with a right hand. He staggered, but didn't go down.

He hit me twice in the ribs, bending me over, then caught me with a glancing blow on the cheek that dropped me. Again I started climbing to my feet.

"Stay . . . down . . . damn you," he gasped.

Everything was blurred, and all I could hear was my own coarse breathing. Murphy swung a left, and I blocked it with more luck than skill. Then I hit him in the ribs three times, backing him up.

A left caught me on the cheek. He tried a second, and I ducked under, then crossed it with a right. I caught him flush and he went down to his knees. I reached for what was left of his shirt, thinking to haul him to his feet, but he waved both hands, shook his head.

" 'Nough," he gasped. "I had enough."

My knees gave out and I dropped right in front of him. For what seemed a long time we sat there, trying to draw air into our lungs. Everything I had hurt like hell, and if my face looked anything like Murphy's, I didn't want to see no mirrors for a month.

Then folks were swarming around, helping us both to our feet. "Whiskey," I said. "I need a whiskey."

"I'll buy it," Murphy said. "If you'll drink it."

"You're a tough man, Murphy. Be damned if you ain't. I'll drink your whiskey."

Folks hustled us into the nearest bar and yelled for a bottle. Murphy took a drink, spat out a jaw tooth. We were both so damned weak we had to lean against the bar for support. Two drinks later, Murphy looked over at me.

"You aren't the best fighter I ever went against," he said, "but you're by God the toughest. Never saw a man keep coming like that."

"You did the same."

"Would you believe me if I said I didn't put Harris up to the trouble he's caused you? The truth is, I fired him two months ago and haven't heard from him since."

It felt like I was speaking through a mouthful of cotton. "Then why'd he do it?"

"Probably thought I'd give him his job back, and maybe a bonus. I might have, too. But I didn't put him up to it."

"I believe you."

Murphy held out his hand, and I shook it. Folks cheered like it was the fourth of July. Then somebody stuck their face up close to mine. "There's a woman outside asking to see you," he said.

"A woman?"

"Yes, sir. A fine-looking one."

I nodded, let go of the bar. I made three steps before my knees gave out. Hands helped me back to my feet. It was Marshal Reynolds had me on one side, and Billy on the other. "You all right?" Marshal Reynolds asked.

"Hell, no, I ain't all right. Murphy hits fit to kill a man."

"He's in every bit as bad a shape as you are. It'd be best if you let me walk you down to see Doctor Jefferies, though. Something might be broken."

"Finding something that ain't broken would be the trick. Reckon it'll all heal."

"I guess."

I walked out of the saloon, and there stood Kate. She was wearing a blue dress, the sun was shining off her hair, and in all my days I'd never seen anything that looked half as good.

She saw me and gasped, then ran right up to me. "Oh, Ben, are you all right?"

"I'm a mite tuckered, but I'll live."

"Just like a man to settle his troubles by fighting. Don't you think you're a little old for this?"

"Yes, ma'am. Only that's how it had to be. I had to whup Murphy or shoot him."

"I guess you went the right way, then. But once we're married, I don't want any more of this."

"Married! You and me?"

"You do want to marry me, don't you? You've been hanging around like a moonstruck calf for months."

"Yes, ma'am, you know I do. Only I never figured you'd be the one doing the asking."

"Well, if I waited for you to ask me, I'd be eighty and too tired to care."

"Yes, ma'am. Might be. I sure wanted to ask, only I didn't know how and figured you'd laugh if I did. Besides, I ain't much, Kate. I drink too much, I cuss something awful, and my manners ain't such as to please most folks."

"Yes, and you fight too much and don't have any more brains than it takes to make it through the day. And you know too much about saloon women; you aren't all that much to look at; and if you ever stepped inside a church, the roof would probably fall in.

"But you're a kind, caring man, Ben Hawkins, and all those other things are just reasons you need a good wife."

"Yes, ma'am. I expect I do."

Kate slipped her arm through mine, and we walked off down the street. And you know what, the moment she touched me, every ache I had drifted off like smoke in the wind.